Rulers of Light

Bethanny Lawson

Dedication

I wrote this book for you. I hope you enjoy this story and that it becomes as much a part of you as it is a part of me.

1

Evelyn laid *The Magician's Nephew* on her chest and breathed in the scent of roses mingled with exhaust fumes and filthy pavement. Although the flower beds crammed into their tiny yard took up much of her hardworking mother's time, Evelyn cherished how they blocked the view of her urban neighborhood. Evelyn's stunning green eyes flashed with a seventeen year old's dream of living in wide open spaces surrounded by deep forests to explore.

And fewer people.

Evelyn closed her eyes. She could practically hear the voice of her busy older brother, spinning vivid stories of imaginary worlds while she fixed her long, flowing waves of silky brown hair into piles on top of her head "like a princess" on many a day passed. Days much like this one.

"Hello."

Evelyn's eyes popped open as she jerked up onto one elbow. A stick figure of a boy was standing over her. Evelyn groaned. Travis.

"What are you doing here?" she demanded.

"Hanging out with you," Travis replied, cheerful as ever.

"Was the gate unlocked?"

Travis shook his head innocently.

"Well, I'm reading," Evelyn huffed, picking up her book and attempting to engross herself in it again.

"Cool!" Travis sat down close to her. He pointed to the title. "I've read this one."

Evelyn pulled the book closer to her face. Travis fell to his back next to her. "Which book in the series is your favorite?" he asked.

Evelyn rolled her eyes. "All of them." She stood abruptly. Travis leapt to his feet after her like greased lightning.

"I'm going inside," Evelyn informed Travis.

"Okay!" Travis replied to her retreating back.

Only when Evelyn reached the door and almost smashed Travis closing it did she realize that the kid had no intention of leaving. Obviously he didn't know how to take a hint. Evelyn lovingly laid her book on a counter and spun towards Travis threateningly.

"You know it's really rude to invite yourself over to..."

The half spoken sentence hung in the air like a thunder cloud when Evelyn's mother entered the kitchen. Evelyn wished she could lead her "friend" back outside, but it was too late.

"Travis! How lovely to see you." Evelyn's mother kicked off her shoes. She had a soft spot for Travis and anyone like him. Evelyn admired the kindness her mother possessed.

"Why don't you stay for dinner?"

But admiration did not lessen Evelyn's irritation.

"Can I?" Travis was thrilled.

"We'd love to have you."

When her mother's back turned, Evelyn glared at Travis. He grinned back at her. She took a deep, cleansing breath and started setting the table.

As Evelyn grudgingly set an extra plate on the table, she felt a tug on her hair. Immediately an arm went around her neck and a two fingered imitation gun was pointing at her head. Evelyn giggled and reached behind her to grab at her brother.

"Nikolai..."

"Sh..." He pulled her in close and whispered in her ear. "Not another word."

"Nik, let your sister go and make yourself useful." Their mother started unwrapping frozen pizzas and turned on the oven.

"Fine." Nikolai released Evelyn.

Travis was happily engaged in conversation with their mother. Catching Evelyn's sigh of relief, Nik leaned on the table and put on his cool kid face. "This guy still pestering you?" he asked, jerking a thumb over his shoulder.

"Yes, very much so."

"Do I need to take care of him for ya?"

Evelyn grinned. "I almost wish you would, but he's nothing more than an annoyance. Harmless, truly."

"Well, just make the best of it then." Nikolai squared his shoulders, looked straight into Evelyn's eyes, and patted her shoulder. "You're probably his only friend."

"Yeah?" she retorted. "Then go be his second friend."

"Don't have to." He smiled mischievously. "You've got this covered." Nik ducked out of the room before Evelyn could throw something at him.

She sighed and looked at Travis. She didn't want to be rude, but no one could handle needy people all of the time.

2

Evelyn's mother asked the kids, including Travis, to help weed the gardens after dinner. Evelyn conveniently disappeared into the very back corner of the garden. Every tugged weed released a bit of Evelyn's tension.

Soon Evelyn came across a weed she had never seen before, a black vine that looked as though it were dead. Momentarily perplexed, Evelyn decided if it was one of her mother's plants, it wasn't much good anymore, so she started tugging at it. The weed resisted.

Then the black vine twisted around Evelyn's wrist and yanked her to the ground, knocking her breath out. Evelyn rubbed her head, sighing in slight annoyance. "What is Nik up to now?" It was the only possible explanation. Nik had outdone himself this time.

Evelyn stared suspiciously at the vine. When she started brushing it off, another vine burst from the soil and encircled her ankle. She jumped, swirled, and tried to tug it off, but the vine around her wrist pulled her back to the ground. A tingle shivered up Evelyn's spine.

When a third vine crept up around her other arm, Evelyn fought against it furiously. This only served to encourage the rapid growth of many more vines, which sprung up out of the soil and twisted around Evelyn, each one bigger than the last. Her voice seemed small, far away. No one could hear her and no one came to save Evelyn from this nightmare.

She squirmed and struggled and screamed to no avail. She no longer cared where these vines came from or how they so cunningly ensnared her, she just wanted out of them.

Soon they covered her entirely. Evelyn felt sick. The ground beneath her shifted and hardened into rock. She felt dizzy, as though everything was spinning out of control.

As quickly as they had covered her, the vines around Evelyn's face parted.

Evelyn was stunned by what lay in front of her. A forest engulfed in darkness contained blackened trees. They looked dead, as though a forest fire had swept through, yet they were most certainly alive. Too alive. They moved, as if in a dance, their branches eerily weaving among one another. Hard black earth stretched, bare and cracked, in the forest's open spaces.

A dark, sinister man stood in front of Evelyn. Not particularly tall, he was frightening nevertheless and matched the scenery well. His eyes gathered her up like some sort of trophy.

"So," he spoke at last. "You've finally come."

Evelyn and the dark man shared a moment of silence. He stared at Evelyn, then gestured for a group of men behind him to chop her loose from the vines.

"Move quickly," the dark man snapped, stepping out to lead. The men instantly scooped Evelyn up and turned to follow him, carrying her inside a massive dark castle. Now she realized the hard surface she had felt at her back was a wall of that castle.

Hallways twisted and turned in every direction. Just when Evelyn predicted they would come to an end, a whole new series would begin. It would be ridiculous to run. If she did get away, what would she do? Where would she go? Evelyn didn't want to guess what else was out there besides the imposing forest. Surely she would be more likely to die out there than she would stuck here in... well... where on earth was she?

Evelyn writhed against the painful grasp on her arm. She was perfectly capable of walking on her own.

Finally the group stepped out onto a balcony above a

massive room with towering ceilings. People, weapons, horses, and various noises and smells filled the room. Evelyn could hardly see to the end of it for all its size and darkness. The torches lining the walls cast just enough light to create a sinister aura. Though Evelyn's senses were mostly overwhelmed, a ghostly sense of fear and evil began to fill her. She needed fresh air. She needed light.

The leader took Evelyn from his men. "Start moving out a small group. I'll follow with her presently."

"Won't the shields go up if they attack us?" one man asked.

"We still need to be prepared to defend ourselves."

The men nodded and filed down the stairs. The leader tightened his grip on Evelyn, who stopped struggling with a yelp. Her captor chuckled.

"We're so glad you have come to Scaolust," he crooned, a snake like grin slithering across his face.

"I don't even know what that is," Evelyn finally spoke, her own voice dripping with irritation.

"Ah." The man only seemed more pleased. "Scaolust is the kingdom of darkness in this world, and I am Virgo, king over the land."

That explanation confused Evelyn even more. Virgo studied her for a moment, then gestured to the crowded room below. "You get used to it eventually."

Evelyn didn't know how to reply so they stood silently for a moment before Virgo pulled her down a narrow flight of stairs that pressed close against the wall. Scraping and clanging, a giant door began to open. A little air—not fresh, yet welcome—swept into the building. The prepared group of men filled the exit and poured from the castle. The exiting platoon was small, but the open door allowed Evelyn to note the vastness of the grand army staying behind.

Virgo mounted the horse standing ready for him. Evelyn was pushed up behind him and they galloped to catch the army.

3

It was hardly a scenic ride. The door had released them straight into the woods. Besides the army, there was nothing alive to be seen, unless the ever moving trees counted as something alive. Evelyn felt just as trapped as she had inside the castle.

Abruptly, the forest ended, giving way to yet another strange sight. A huge, imposing, single flower sprouted from the earth. It came up to Evelyn's waist and was almost as wide as it was tall.

Yet its size wasn't that strange. The strange thing was how the flower was split perfectly into two distinct halves. One half was the darkest blue, gray, and purple, just barely not black like its center. The stem and leaves of that half of the flower were the darkest dark green.

The other half of the flower had a light green stem, a bright yellow center, and pink, peach, and yellow petals. The bright half was delicate and cheerful, the other half was obtrusive and offensive. Each side contrasted with the other in every way.

The dark half of the flower was in Scaolust, but where the dark half ended, so did Scaolust. The light half of the flower was in a place as beautiful as itself. A vast meadow splashed with the colors of thousands of flowers stretched away from the split flower and away from Evelyn. To the right, the dark forest also changed. Trees were split down the middle like the flower. Leaves of rich green dazzled in the dappled light that filtered through onto the healthy brown earth, while the other half stood scorched and scalded black.

It was as though the flower divided two entirely different worlds. Awe filled Evelyn as she observed the beauty of the other land.

At Virgo's command, Evelyn was dragged off the horse and tied roughly to a tree, which she could feel moving under her. She wiggled uncomfortably. The ropes were pulled tighter and she sighed in exasperation.

4

At the sounds of battle, Evelyn snapped her head up just in time to see Virgo's men clash with another group rushing from the other side of the flower. Despite his precautions, Virgo was being steadily advanced upon by a smaller army.

A young man with not quite curly black hair, about Evelyn's age or even a little younger, led the attackers. He was a striking young man, full of life. He broke away from the battle and directed his horse to where Evelyn was bound. He leapt down and began efficiently slicing through the ropes restraining her. As he cut through the final thread, he took Evelyn's hand.

"Hurry," his amber eyes flashed urgency as he scurried back up his horse and swung Evelyn up behind him.

The horse started moving just as Virgo was upon them. Swords glinted in the approaching sunlight and clashed a few times before Evelyn and the boy were safely away.

The boy called out to his men, who obediently retreated to the meadow.

"Are you alright?" the boy asked Evelyn, kindness etched on his face. She nodded, so he smiled, satisfied, and let the horse run.

The combined galloping of the horses made a thundering rhythm in the ground, music that could be felt but not replicated. Waves rippled through the meadow, the tall grass bowing to them as they swept by. Evelyn held the boy tightly and leaned her head against the back of his shoulder, struggling not to fall off, but thoroughly enjoying the ride.

Another spectacular castle came into sight. Its huge towers rose into the sky, the walls constructed of the most beautiful gray brick. Wide doors swung open, welcoming them, as the boy pulled his horse to a halt.

He jumped down nimbly, then reached up to help Evelyn dismount. She felt lighter than air when he lifted her, displaying impressive strength for his age.

The boy led her forward and Evelyn followed him willingly. She involuntarily gasped at the beauty before her, everything seeming to glow of vibrant colors. Too distracted to pay attention to where she was being led, Evelyn stopped at massive wooden doors tinted with gold and covered with intricate engravings. The boy pushed the heavy double doors open and strode forward with confidence.

Evelyn was struck motionless. Magnificent sunlight streamed through tall windows behind three thrones, casting a magical glow over the room. Warmth exuded from the place.

Evelyn's escort nudged her with his elbow. She followed him obediently.

Someone rose from the center throne as the boy and Evelyn approached him. He was a young man, his hair the color of the golden autumn sun. His pure, crystal blue eyes sparkled and his fair skin glowed with health. Exactly the opposite of Virgo in every way, he smiled warmly at Evelyn, and an incomprehensible shiver went down her spine.

"We are so glad you have finally come." He beckoned the two forward and greeted them with a bow. "I am king Rennigan of Heretrua." He fixed his gaze directly on Evelyn. "But, as I am certain we will become friends during your stay, please just call me Ren."

Motioning towards the boy who had brought Evelyn in, Ren introduced him. "This is my brother, Prince Ty." The boy nodded to Evelyn, grinning. "And this," Ren smiled fondly as he motioned for someone to the side to step forward, "Is my sister, Princess Jacquelyn."

His sister was the picture of serenity and simplicity. She

had glowing auburn eyes and hair that matched them. Good looks obviously ran in the family. Jacquelyn acknowledged Evelyn with a soft nod.

"So," Ren continued curiously. "What made you decide to come at last?"

"Decide?" Evelyn's voice stuck, so she tried again. "I didn't really decide, I was just... pulled here. By vines. I don't even know how it happened." Evelyn peered at Ren suspiciously. "Why was I brought here?"

Ren smiled again. "I'm sorry. We had assumed that you would come knowingly. Willingly. We forgot the possibility that you might be forced here." His eyebrows scrunched inward in thought. "What is your name?"

Her face warmed. "I'm Evelyn."

"Evelyn..." Ren repeated her name aloud and nodded, as if taking it in. All at once, Evelyn loved her name. It sounded regal, important. "Well, Evelyn. We're glad that you have come to our world, whether it was of your own choosing or not. You are joyfully welcomed here." Ty nodded enthusiastically at this. Ren shared a knowing look with him. Both pairs of eyes flashed.

"I'm assuming you didn't harm anyone?" Ren questioned Ty.

Ty shook his head. "Would I be here if I had?"

Evelyn couldn't make sense of this. "Why don't you want to hurt any of them? Aren't they the enemy?"

Ren turned his attention back to Evelyn. "It's the flower. You don't know anything about that either?"

Evelyn shook her head.

"It divides the kingdoms of Scaolust and Heretrua. It protects them from each other. If one kingdom attacks and harms the other, the flower puts up a barrier between the kingdoms."

"That is one special flower," Evelyn commented.

"I'll say," Ty spoke up.

Evelyn looked at him for further explanation. "How exactly does it do that?"

Ty just shrugged.

"That flower holds the key to who will gain ultimate reign of the realm," Ren continued.

"How?" Evelyn asked.

"When it is picked, the side it is picked from will rule, and the other side will be utterly destroyed."

"How is that possible? And why hasn't someone picked it yet?"

"It isn't that simple." Jacquelyn spoke for the first time. "Legend tells that someone from another world will be the one chosen to pick it. This person must be neutral to both kingdoms." She emphasized her last sentence.

Evelyn tried to fit the pieces together in her head. "This flower alone holds power over two kingdoms, is protecting them from each other, and is impossible to pick?" Jacquelyn and Ren shared a look and Ty simply shrugged. "Where'd this thing come from?"

"So much information has been lost through the years," Ren explained to her. "All we really know is its purpose."

"Which is?"

"To make sure fate is decided by a worthy judge beyond the situation."

Evelyn suddenly realized why she had been so important to Virgo, why Ty had lead an attack against Virgo to free her, and why she was standing here now before the King of Heretrua. Why she had been pulled to this world at all. "That's *my* job?"

Ren nodded. "Now that you've arrived, we have reason to hope. We're in a weak condition right now, for reasons that take too long to explain. Scaolust is by far the stronger kingdom and will overthrow us without the flower's protection."

"But now you're here," Jacquelyn stepped forward. "And we know you'll choose right."

"We still have to watch out," Ty warned. "Scaolust's done a pretty good job dividing the light without sending up the barrier these past few hundred years." He threw Ren a dirty glance. The king ignored it. "Time's running down and they know it."

"What do you mean by, 'time's running down?'"

"If we don't pick the flower at exactly the right moment, its power will be lost. Our job is to protect you until then."

"How will I know when to pick it?"

"The flower wants to be picked," Jacquelyn said. "By the right person. You'll be drawn to it at the appropriate time."

Evelyn couldn't help but giggle. "How convenient that the flower has the loudest opinion in the matter."

The king noticed the bruises on Evelyn's arms. "Oh! I'm so sorry." He moved his hand in a downward motion in Evelyn's direction. "Scaolust is not a kind kingdom."

For a brief moment a white glow flowed from his hand, a white shimmer passed over Evelyn, and her bruises disappeared. Evelyn stared at her arms, then at Rennigan, shocked.

"What did you just do?" she demanded.

Ren laughed. "No magic in your world, is there?"

"Magic?"

At that moment, the sound of opening doors caused Evelyn to whirl around. A commanding figure stepped in. She had red hair pulled up sharply to the top of her head and wore a deep red dress, its plunging neckline emphasized by a heavy necklace. Her steel gray eyes stared Evelyn down as she approached Ren.

"Evelyn," Ren's voice took on a different tone. "This is Philomena."

Both girls studied each other critically. Philomena eventually turned coldly away.

Ty met Philomena's eyes with a wary gaze. Philomena slipped her hand into Ren's elbow and somehow the look she exchanged with Ren stung Evelyn.

Jacquelyn stepped down and hooked her elbow in Evelyn's as if they had been best friends their whole lives. "I'll get you comfortable here," she said. "I'm sure you're exhausted by now." She glanced to her older brother for approval, and Ren nodded.

Jacquelyn and Evelyn left the other three to themselves. As the backs of the two girls disappeared, Philomena turned to Ren. "Who is she?"

"She's the one." He squeezed her hand. "She's going to save us."

5

Jacquelyn took Evelyn down halls and up stairs until she was thoroughly lost.

"I knew castles were big, but they seem even bigger once you're inside," Evelyn commented.

Jacquelyn giggled and turned her head to look at Evelyn. "You're going to want to get cleaned up, aren't you?"

Evelyn looked down at herself. "I haven't had time to think about it, but that would be nice."

"You can come borrow something of mine to wear while your rooms are being prepared. I'll have some dresses made for you tomorrow."

"I don't want to put you to any trouble."

Jacquelyn waved a hand, "It's no trouble."

"I'm not going to be here long, am I?"

Jacquelyn looked at Evelyn. "What do you mean?"

"Well, won't I go back home when this is all over?"

"Oh." Jacquelyn shrugged. "I'm sorry, I really have no idea. Even if you are going home, we don't know how long you'll have to wait on the flower."

They had apparently reached their destination. Jacquelyn stopped and opened a door. "Come in."

As Jacquelyn sorted through her clothing, things fell too silent for Evelyn.

"So... Philomena isn't related to you?"

"No." Jacquelyn offered no further explanation.

"What's she doing here then? Where is she from?"

"Scaolust."

Evelyn blinked. "Scaolust?"

"Yes." Jacquelyn sighed and turned towards Evelyn. "Virgo is her grandfather. Her story is that she escaped the darkness and came to us."

"And?"

"And what?"

"You don't seem overly fond of her."

"I don't trust her. If your brother was king and courting someone from Scaolust in a time of war, would you trust that person?"

Evelyn was quiet as Jacquelyn helped her into a nightgown. So Philomena *was* special to Ren.

"I'll show you to your rooms now," Jacquelyn told Evelyn. "Get some rest. If you need anything, don't hesitate to ask." She smiled. "After all, you are an honored guest here."

Evelyn was completely willing to crawl into the bed provided for her and bury herself deep in the blankets, hiding from the confusion and exhaustion pushing in on her. Maybe she'd feel less like she was a small child again when she woke up.

6

The following morning, Rennigan endlessly paced the floor of the throne room. His feet were sore, but he couldn't bring himself to stop moving.

They were so close to freedom. Everything rested on Evelyn. There was no single action Ren could take to speed up the process or to ensure it went smoothly. His worry wasn't whether or not Evelyn would make the right choice, it was his lack of control that bothered him.

It is one thing to be young, and another thing entirely to be young and clueless. Evelyn was both. She knew nothing of the land and had no method of defending herself.

Still, what could go wrong?

Ty watched, amused, from his throne. He sat in it sideways, his feet propped up on the arms, looking entirely laid back, amiable, and content.

"You're going to need new shoes," he commented. Ren couldn't help but crack a small grin at his brother. He wished he could be as confident and carefree as Ty was.

Philomena leaned with one arm against a wall, dazzling, even in the shadows. To Ren Philomena was a treasure, a resting place—his last hope for a normal life. A welcome distraction.

Ren finally stopped pacing and sat on a step. "I don't like waiting," he declared. "We have no idea what Scaolust is planning. We have no way to protect her."

"Planning?" Ty raised one eyebrow. "What would they be planning? They're probably panicking. That's what I would do."

"You would not."

Philomena moved to Ren's side, and crouched next to him, placing calming hands on his shoulders. "I don't think it's worth so much of your worry."

"But this girl and this flower hold the future of our kingdom." Ren gazed up at her. "If we lose either, we lose everything."

Ty swung his legs off the arm of his throne and stood up. "It's a waste of time to worry. We have no control anyway."

"Exactly. That's what bothers me!" Ren threw his hands in the air in frustration.

"Calm down, Ren. Virgo couldn't take Evelyn back without harming our kingdom, and he couldn't get in without us knowing. The flower will protect us from him. Is there really any way for Scaolust to win?"

Ren pondered this a moment. "They're good at getting around the rules. I just feel like they'll find a way."

Philomena spoke up again. "Ty's right."

Ty nodded firmly. "Thank you."

Philomena smiled. She tried to catch Ren's gaze. "Hey." He looked up at her and she took both of his hands. "There's no way Virgo can ruin this for us."

He shook his head and broke away from her gaze again.

"Are you sure?" Jacquelyn ventured. "They have always found ways to cause trouble before."

Philomena threw her head around and silenced Jacquelyn with a look. Ren sighed, dropped Philomena's hands, and started pacing again. Philomena joined Jacquelyn and cautiously put an arm around her shoulders. "Let him have peace," she whispered.

7

When Evelyn found the castle ballroom, she stopped worrying about whether or not she should be exploring without permission.

It was every bit as magical as stories made ballrooms seem. Evelyn slowly made her way across the dance floor to the edge of the balcony and found herself looking over the meadow, the forest to the left side. It would have been the most beautiful view of any land, if it wasn't for the black shadow that washed over it, and the definite line where light ended and evil began. If Evelyn strained her eyes, she could barely see Virgo's group gathered by the flower.

What were they still there for, anyway?

Evelyn spotted a telescope. She knew how to use that. Back home, her dad took her out into the country and taught her how to use his telescope for star gazing. This couldn't be much different.

Virgo was standing at the very edge of Scaolust like there was an invisible wall that prevented him from stepping foot into Heretrua. On the other side of the division, a young lady stood conversing with Virgo passionately.

As the lady turned to walk away, Evelyn focused the telescope on the figure in order to see her face clearly. It was Philomena.

What was she doing?

Virgo held up his hands, and as darkness filled them, Evelyn remembered Jacquelyn telling her that all royalty had magic. That must include royalty of Scaolust.

Fear struck through Evelyn's heart like a knife as Virgo shot black magic into the ground. Jagged cracks broke the ground and black vines grew out of them, pushing through to Heretrua's land.

The vines stopped moving and Virgo stopped using his magic. Evelyn sighed in relief.

Another burst of darkness, from Heretrua's side this time, caught Evelyn's eye. Philomena began pulling the black vines further into Heretrua with her own magic.

She had magic. She had dark magic. But that wasn't the worst of it.

Evelyn had to warn Rennigan.

Philomena stopped using her magic, and the darkness continued forward on its own, advancing into the kingdom of light. Philomena turned around, satisfied, and started back towards Heretrua's castle. Evelyn watched her gaze travel up the castle and freeze on the telescope. Evelyn gasped and lurched backward.

Evelyn was halfway down the staircase when everything in front of her exploded into blackness. A cold, harsh wind knocked her to the ground. When Evelyn rubbed the darkness from her eyes and looked up, Philomena was standing on the stairs in front of her, a victorious smile on her face.

"They had such great faith in you," she crooned. Evelyn climbed backwards, scrambling to get to her feet. Philomena grasped Evelyn with her magic. "They've waited so long. You were going to save them all."

"You can't do anything about it," Evelyn spoke fiercely. "The flower won't allow you to harm us."

Philomena laughed. "Silly child, I'm not going to hurt you. We need you alive just as much as they do. The only difference is that now..." The black magic appeared in Philomena's hands again and rose around Evelyn. "They'll die by *your* hand."

The magic rose, swirled, and blocked everything else out. The whirlwind pinned Evelyn down; she couldn't even open her eyes. Everything was blackness. Evelyn couldn't think and everything slowly faded away.

8

Philomena's footsteps became purposeful and quick. Now only one thought consumed her.

She found Ren alone with his worries. He turned around brightly at the sound he easily recognized as Philomena's footsteps.

"Philomena, I was hoping to see you..." his sentence faded, morphing into suspicion. "What's wrong? Is it Evelyn? The flower?"

"All is well," Philomena replied. "I'm sorry for disturbing you. I just wanted to catch you alone."

She placed a seductive smile on her face, closed the doors firmly, and stepped forward. "Things have been so tense lately that we haven't gotten any time alone together, just you and me." She leaned into him, looking up into his face, playing innocent. He grinned at her.

"You're feeling affectionate today," he teased. Philomena giggled and made him sit in a chair. She sat on the arm herself.

"It makes for a more entertaining story."

"Unfortunately, we don't live in a story," Ren softly replied.

"Are you sure about that?" Philomena moved her hand behind Ren's head and mingled her fingers with his hair. "After all, don't all the best stories have hardships?"

He smiled and put a hand over hers. "In that case, our story is going to be the greatest of them all."

"Only if you make it great."

"How do you want me to do that?"

"Let me teach you," Philomena implored. "While it's just you and me." She leaned on his shoulder. "You never know when we'll get time like this again."

"Well then," he smiled and sat back. "Teach me."

Philomena smiled. "Close your eyes."

Ren obeyed.

"Now what makes a great story? It could be the plot or the action. But what makes the best stories, our story, great?" Philomena paused a moment. "Can you guess?"

Ren shook his head.

"It's the characters." She fitted her fingers between his. "The way they interact and intersect."

"But no matter how good the characters are," Ren chimed in, "if there's no happy ending, the story makes me feel robbed of something."

Philomena giggled and nudged him playfully. "No cliffhangers for you?"

"No."

"Very well then. Write the epilogue."

"Now?"

"Yes, now."

Ren opened his eyes. "We'll have time for what really matters when it's all over. Time for my people. Time for my siblings. Time for appreciating the beauty in simple things." He looked up at Philomena, playfulness dancing in his eyes. "Time for love," he said.

Philomena smiled. "Well then, in that case," she continued. "You're going to have to prove your love in the rest of the story." She grinned at him mischievously. "How are you going to accomplish that?"

"How?" Contemplating, Ren smiled. "I think you know how."

Philomena was close enough to his face to see the detail of his blue eyes and to feel the warmth of his breath. She smiled and closed her eyes, exhaling slowly. "I do," she whispered. "But I want something bigger."

"What is that?" he was so close, so ready.

She let out a little breathy laugh. "Plot twist."

Philomena pulled vines through the windows behind the throne so fast Ren didn't see it coming. They wrapped around Ren and held him down. Philomena leapt to her feet and backed away. Ren looked up at her, then to her hands, where blackness was fading away.

"Philomena, what are you doing?"

Philomena smiled in the purest satisfaction. "You're so foolish Rennigan."

Ren's own hands filled with light. Philomena simply laughed at him and lifted a few fingers.

The vines began to move again, tightening around the king. Ren felt a tugging sensation from deep within and the light drained out of his hand. He couldn't bring it back. The magic was being pulled from him into the vines. He grew weaker and weaker, and finally all the magic had been pulled from him.

Gasping for breath, Ren could barely hold his head up. It was as if a part of him had been ripped out. The corner of Philomena's mouth turned up. A ball of glowing light floated at the tip of a vine. She approached it, and took it in her hand, absorbing it into herself.

Ren pulled weakly against the vines as Philomena used two fingers to stroke his cheek. "Coulda been something, huh Ren?"

He glared at her, completely helpless. She pulled a dagger out and crouched next to him, holding it close to his face so he could see it clearly. "Heretrua wouldn't last long even with you."

At that moment, the shields shot up from the flower around both kingdoms, pulling Philomena away from Heretrua, safely away from Ren, and back into Scaolust where she belonged, leaving the king alone.

Ren hung his head and sighed. "Ty's gonna kill me."

Cold wind came in through the shattered windows, harsh, dark wind all the way from Scaolust, and dimmed the room. Evil was already filtering its way in.

Philomena was more powerful than Ren would have ever expected. How could she take away his magic? That was unheard of.

How many times had the brothers argued over this exact issue? How many times had Jacquelyn expressed her fears? And yet, Philomena always managed to make the naysayers appear as raving lunatics to Ren.

But only to Ren.

9

Jacquelyn and Ty burst in on their brother at the same time.

"What happened?" Jacquelyn asked as a bit of amethyst light spiraled out of her fingertips and Rennigan was freed from the vines. She knelt by her brother and studied him inquisitively, concern written across her face.

"And why didn't you just use your own magic to fix this?" Ty finished for Jacquelyn. A blast of azure filled the room, and all the vines snaked out the windows, which quickly repaired themselves. Ty slapped his hands together proudly. "I think the windows look better than they did before." Jacquelyn rolled her eyes.

"I can't," Ren responded, as he stood up and started making his way towards the doors. "She took my magic."

"Who is she?" Ty asked, running to catch up with his brother's long strides. "What's going on?"

"Took your magic? And it hasn't refilled like it normally does?"

"It's not like that this time." Ren didn't answer Ty's question. "Is everyone else in the castle safe?"

"As far as we know," Jacquelyn responded. "But we didn't even know you were in trouble until now. Ren, who did this to you? And why?"

Ty put a firm hand on Ren's shoulder to stop him. "Let us help," he pleaded. "Look, I know it has to be someone else with magic, and our only enemies are from Scaolust." He raised his eyebrows in suspicion. "Got anything to tell us?"

Ren knew he had to start talking eventually, and sooner was probably better. "Philomena," he admitted.

Ty's expression hardened. "I've tried to warn you about this before."

33

Ren waved him off. "I know, Ty."

Ty exploded. "If you had listened we wouldn't have a problem now. If you weren't so stubborn…"

"You're no different!"

"But I'm right more often than you!"

"I know that, but can't you see I'm wallowing in enough guilt as it is?"

"Just admit the truth."

"Why, so you can say 'I told you so?'"

"You've taken my advice on everything else before," the prince continued, sounding a bit hurt. "It's insulting to think Philomena took a higher place in your life than your brother."

Jacquelyn put a hand on each of her brother's shoulders. "Ty, calm down. We have a bigger enemy to defeat than we have time for."

Ren didn't break eye contact with Ty. "I'm sorry. I know you were right, but what do you want me to do about it now?"

Ty shrugged. "Fix it." He narrowed his eyes. "Take my advice and help this time."

Ren managed a small smile. "I will. And you know, had I ever been forced to choose between you and Philomena, which one it would it be."

"I hope so."

"Come on, you'll always come first."

"And always be right," Ty gloated. Jacquelyn kicked him.

"Hey!" Ty protested. "That's abusive!"

A thought came to Ren's head, and any feeling of relief drained out of him. "Where's Evelyn?"

Jacquelyn went white. "Oh no."

Ty was already gone. The trio raced upstairs and burst into Evelyn's room. She wasn't there. They ordered servants to search the castle, and found that Evelyn was gone.

As soon as the siblings set out for Scaolust, they could see the shields the flower had put up.

Ren looked at Ty. "Now would be a great time for some brilliancy out of you."

10

Evelyn's view in Scaolust was dismal. Heretrua was silent and still and Evelyn's life was spinning in front of her.

There was no escape. What would happen to her after the flower was picked? What use would Scaolust have for her?

The aftermath of picking the flower hadn't looked like a problem when she was in Heretrua.

Evelyn didn't see the point in fighting. If she was to get past the army, she would have to get through two impenetrable walls. Everything seemed hopeless.

This wasn't fair. If she was intended to be the judge, she should have the ability to go back and forth between both kingdoms at will. With all the magic in this world, why had this not been taken care of?

Commotion filled the air. Evelyn looked up to see Virgo make his way through his armies to the wall between the two kingdoms.

Jacquelyn and Ty were combining their magic in a valiant effort to break through the walls while Ren watched, still powerless. Virgo smiled, folded his arms, and observed, locking eyes with Ren.

You've already lost, Virgo told the other king with his eyes.

Virgo glanced at Evelyn, who was looking at the wall hopefully. He chuckled, and she swung to look at him. "What are you so excited about?"

Evelyn opened her mouth to answer, then stopped and simply scowled at Virgo. He gestured behind him. "This doesn't change anything."

Evelyn still refused to reply, only stared past him towards Heretrua.

When the king of Scaolust turned back to his armies to

start giving orders, the expressions on their faces stopped him. They started yelling at their leader to turn around, look behind him, and there were hundreds of fingers pointing over his head.

Virgo turned back around to see a small hole only about the size of his fist, but progressively growing larger, in the walls between the two kingdoms.

A growl of frustration came from Virgo as he turned and countered Heretrua's magic with his own. The hole collapsed at first, but Ty and Jacquelyn pushed harder, and it began to form again.

Virgo continued to counter the power until finally the hole froze. It wasn't getting bigger. But it wasn't getting smaller either. The two kingdoms were latched in silent battle.

At that moment, the flower began to glow, gently, quietly, but noticeably. Evelyn felt herself standing up. She could barely feel her feet moving, the ground underneath her, but she knew she was moving. Evelyn tried to turn back, but she had no control. She only progressed towards the flower.

11

All three with magic doubled their efforts when Evelyn started moving. Ren watched anxiously.

Heretrua slowly gained an advantage. The hole had grown big enough for a person to fit through at this point.

Ren looked at Ty. "What do we do now?"

"If you could get Evelyn, that would be great."

"How do you expect me to do that?"

"Not by standing here."

Ren looked at the wall, then at Evelyn moving towards the flower. "Alright." He started forward.

Enraged, Virgo let his hold on the wall go, and it instantly expanded as quick as a wild fire. He wasn't going to let them get through. Even if the wall was open, they wouldn't get through.

Virgo threw a ball of black magic at Ren. It struck his leg and exploded on impact, throwing Ren backwards. For a moment Heretrua could not be seen through the blackness that filled the air.

In that moment of surprise, Virgo attacked the wall again. The hole began collapsing, and Ren's siblings fell back, struggling to keep up their efforts.

Ren, pain crossing his face and filling his eyes, motioned wildly and yelled at his siblings to keep the hole open. They poured their strength into it. Once again the hole froze, open.

Philomena pushed her way through Scaolust's army and joined Virgo at the wall. When she added her own magic to Virgo's, Jacquelyn and Ty were overwhelmed. There was no way they could keep the opening from eventually closing.

Ren pulled himself to his feet and grabbed Ty's shoulder for support. "This isn't working."

"I've noticed." Ty looked at his brother and Ren saw a

glimmer of what was almost defeat in his eyes. "What do you want me to do?"

Ty couldn't look like that. It wasn't over. Ren assessed the two gloating rulers of Scaolust. "You have to get Philomena over here," Ren demanded.

"Are you nuts?"

"Ty, I have to get my magic back!"

"You don't know how to do that."

"It doesn't matter, it's our last chance."

"It can't be."

"Just get her over here!"

"Only if I can kill her once I've got her."

"You want to do that?"

"Yes!" Ty glared up at Ren. "Just because I've never executed anyone before doesn't mean I wouldn't love to start with her."

"If she's dead will I be able to get my magic back?"

Ty stared at Ren for a long time, his expression never changing, "Fine." He looked to Jacquelyn. "Can you keep the wall open?"

The princess looked doubtful, but she nodded and pushed harder. Ty surrounded Philomena with his magic and drug her through the wall to Heretrua.

She smiled at Ty like a satisfied cat. "Hello again, brother."

He grabbed her arm. "You have a lot of nerve," he muttered. She winced, trying not to give him the pleasure of knowing he was starting to hurt her. He grinned. "I can do a lot to you without killing you."

"Now you're starting to sound like one of us." Philomena nodded towards Evelyn. "But you don't have time."

"Ty..." Jacquelyn was struggling. Ren looked impatient. Ty threw Philomena at Ren and grudgingly turned his attention back to the wall.

Philomena stood and smiled at Ren. "Did you want to say a last goodbye?"

"It is goodbye," he replied. "But not for me."

"For the whole kingdom?"

"For one kingdom, yes."

She lifted her hands and Ren grabbed her wrists as magic began to swirl.

"You wouldn't harm me," she said.

"Wouldn't I?"

"I know you wouldn't." she grinned. "You've let me play with too much of your heart, Ren."

"Maybe that's true," Ren agreed, folding his fingers around hers, never taking his eyes off hers.

"What does it feel like?" she whispered. "Having me back like this?"

Ren let out a small laugh. "Fake."

"I was always fake."

"I know. Fake enough that you still don't know the real me. So you see? I do still have an advantage."

Philomena shot the magic from her hands into Ren's, which was exactly what Ren had wanted. He didn't let go, and her surprise showed. Ren's magic, though mingled with Philomena's, poured back into his body eagerly.

Confused, Philomena pushed harder, determined to beat him. Ren was steadfast and determined. She did not recognize what she was accomplishing. Though the pain was intense, the more magic Philomena pushed into Ren, the more magic of his he gained back. A cloud of darkness built up around them.

Ty was anxious. "Ren, let go!"

Ren ignored his brother. He finally had enough magic back to pull his out of her himself. Now Philomena recognized what he was doing. She tried to break away, but his grasp was too strong. Their eyes met and for the first time she looked afraid of him.

Meanwhile, Evelyn was still on a steady course towards the flower. Virgo filled with glee as the rulers of Heretrua began to panic. Evelyn already burned with guilt and despised herself for being unable to stay away from the flower.

With a concentrated effort, Ren pulled the rest of his magic back in one strong tug. In a single motion he shoved Philomena aside and hit Virgo with a powerful burst of light, striking him to the ground.

Wiping the dust off her dress, Philomena smiled. "Ah, but you still won't hurt me, will you Ren?" she murmured to herself.

Philomena stunned Jacquelyn with a burst of magic, causing her to gasp and lose her hold on the wall. Ty turned to help his sister, and the hole collapsed entirely.

A few more steps and Evelyn would reach the flower.

In a burst of black magic, Philomena took herself back to Scaolust, leaving the siblings disorganized and desperate. Evelyn began to reach out for the flower unwillingly, her fingers just inches away.

A burst of blinding light threw everyone on both sides to the ground. People covered their eyes, crying out from the sudden overwhelming power surging through the air. The light hit Evelyn directly on her hands and pushed her away from the flower. The force of the flower was still pulling her, but Ren's magic was holding out against it.

Virgo and Philomena were powerless, blinded by the light. Evelyn, the only one in Scaolust who could see, watched the flower begin to wilt. It was already dying.

Jacquelyn and Ty combined their magic and put

everything in them into forming a hole in the wall one more time, unopposed. The three siblings pulled Evelyn back to Heretrua's side and dropped their magic, exhausted.

Evelyn was instantly pulled to the flower from Heretrua's side and picked it.

For a moment, nothing happened. Both kingdoms froze, waiting. A brief sigh of relief rose from Scaolust, one of defeat in Heretrua. Then silence.

A wave of light rose past where anyone could see, far beyond Heretrua, and swept over all the land, washing through Scaolust, shoving the darkness back. Everything dark and evil was shattered. In one moment, everything was taken from Scaolust.

Scaolust's ground transformed into meadow, its forest grew shrubbery, its trees took on healthy form and sprouted leaves.

Ren and Ty picked Evelyn up off the ground so she could see what she had done. Jacquelyn joined them and the four of them leaned on each other, too weary and happy to speak. Evelyn felt blessed to be a part of this warm, comforting circle of silent celebration.

The transforming wash of light continued right up to the doorstep of the Scaolust castle, then stopped. The four stood waiting for the change to continue. But it never did. The Scaolust castle remained where it was, dark and imposing as it had always been.

"Why isn't it going away?" Evelyn asked wearily.

"Because the flower started dying," Ren sighed.

Evelyn looked up into the king's face. She had disappointed him. All of them. Peace could not last as long as any part of Scaolust remained or any of its leaders were alive.

Ty noticed Evelyn's dismay and knew what she was

thinking. "Evelyn, you did all anyone could ask you to do," he gently insisted.

Evelyn realized it was Ren's arm around her when he tightened it in reassurance. "We're all still here," he said. "That's all that matters."

The four turned back to their own castle and slowly made their way home.

12

Everyone kept to themselves the rest of that day. If they weren't sleeping, they wished they were asleep. Evelyn was restless all night. When she finally did fall asleep, she was plagued with nightmares. Morning couldn't come fast enough.

At last morning did come. All the events of the day before seemed blurry. Evelyn was still coming to grips with what she'd actually seen and done.

Evelyn had felt close to the royal siblings of Heretrua after fighting and winning a battle with them. Now that it was all over, now that Evelyn had fulfilled her purpose, she was a little bit apprehensive about the three siblings again, in awe of them. Could she really have any kind of close bond with people who had been through so much together already when she'd only known them for a few days? Were the relationships even worth building, or would Evelyn be pulled back to her own world at any moment?

Evelyn rolled over to find Jacquelyn sitting in a chair reading a book, patiently waiting for Evelyn to get out of bed.

"Good morning, Evelyn," she said cheerfully. "I came to help you get ready."

Jacquelyn seemed pretty chipper. Too chipper. It bothered Evelyn. "What are you so happy about?" she asked groggily.

"You defeated Scaolust, Evelyn."

Evelyn peered at Jacquelyn through heavy eyelids. "I did not."

"The castle may still be there, but throughout the kingdom, there is celebrating. Our people don't realize the danger is still present, therefore we will ignore it for the time being to best serve our people."

"But wouldn't it be better to serve them by warning them that their lives could be taken at any-"

"The people of Heretrua haven't had anything to celebrate in years. They need joy, not more worry. Now come on," Jacquelyn pulled Evelyn out of bed. "Let's get you dressed!"

Jacquelyn escorted Evelyn to the throne room after making her presentable. "Ren wanted to see you," she said, pulling the doors open for Evelyn.

Evelyn walked through the doors and realized Jacquelyn was closing them behind her, leaving her alone with Ren.

The king, illuminated by glorious sunshine, was sitting on a window sill, looking outside. Evelyn had never talked to Ren alone before, and now that her mission was accomplished she didn't know how to approach him.

Not wanting to startle or interrupt him, she waited for some time before she finally spoke. "Jacquelyn said you wanted to see me."

Ren turned his head, a light smile crossed his face where there had only a few seconds earlier been creases of distress. "Yes, I did," he replied. "You have done us a great service. I want to thank you."

Evelyn didn't know whether to be polite or ask for the truth. She certainly didn't want to be ignorant or to be perceived as such.

"Well, I didn't really have a choice in the matter and the castle is still there," she pointed out. "So I didn't really do anything, did I?"

Ren paused for a moment, then sighed. "You make it hard to compliment you."

"Better the compliments be few and far between and sincere than often and false." Now she was being far too forward.

"That's an excellent point." Ren came closer and looked

Evelyn directly in the eye. "You *have* helped us. Scaolust has less ground now. You've given our people something to celebrate at long last."

"But?"

"But it is true that so long as Scaolust is here, or a ruler alive, we are still in great danger."

"What are you going to do now?" Evelyn asked.

"That is a rather complicated matter," Ren said. He pulled his eyebrows together in thought.

"If I'm asking you to tell me too much..." Evelyn started, but he waved her off.

"No, it's fine." He looked at her. "You're different," he said, as if seeing her clearly for the first time.

Evelyn protested, "I'm just an ordinary human being."

Ren smiled musingly. "Aren't we all?" He stood looking at her for a moment until she gestured towards his leg, concerned.

"You've been limping."

"Virgo's magic," he answered.

"What exactly did he do to it?"

Ren considered, then pulled up his pant leg to show her a mass of black on his leg. The mass looked alive, like it was eating away at the leg itself. Evelyn felt sick looking at it.

"Why can't you heal it like you did to me?" Evelyn asked.

"Virgo injured me with magic," Ren explained. "Our magic cannot influence dark magic. But the darkness always influences the light. It's been a nuisance in far greater affairs than this injury."

"I can imagine." There were so many questions about this place piling up in Evelyn's brain. She didn't understand anything. It was like learning to read all over again. "So if you cannot influence dark magic, how are you ever going to defeat Scaolust?"

Ren shook his head. "That's the problem. We don't have the answer with us yet. We have the normal ways to fight, with weapons and soldiers, but we're not well prepared enough in those areas right now. We are almost completely helpless against all of Scaolust's attacks. Plus, they have another one of their rulers back now."

"Philomena." Ren nodded, but Evelyn knew she was getting into dangerous territory now. She had no right to ask or know anything about this. However, it turned out she didn't have to ask. Ren was defensive and wanted to explain

"I thought I could change her," he insisted. "She made me believe that she had really left the darkness behind."

"That's perfectly logical."

"But it's never happened before."

"What hasn't?"

"Darkness never changes. You can't fix it, you can only fight back."

"Then why did you let your guard down?"

"I hoped I might have a small a piece of a normal life."

"But you did love her."

"Was it love?" he turned to look Evelyn in the eye again. "I thought it was. Looking back now I know it wasn't. It was so fake, so completely out of my character. I was desperate for a distraction. I wanted things to be easier, and she made it look so easy."

They were silent for a moment. Evelyn had been wondering about something, so she asked Ren. "What happens to me now?"

"What do you mean?"

"What good am I? I've done my job, the flower is gone."

"You're still every bit as welcome here."

"And I appreciate that, but what about home? Will I ever go back?"

"Ah. The only way you'll be able to go home is if you get pulled back the way you were pulled here. None of us can send you back. I'm sorry. We will do our very best to make you feel at home here, though I know it won't ever be the same."

Evelyn nodded. Emotions flooded her heart. She was sure she would love sharing life with this family. She was grateful for their generosity. Getting comfortable around them wasn't difficult. But grieving the loss of her own family would take time.

And then there was Ren. She was still in awe of him. He demanded respect and as king was more formal than his siblings out of habit. Evelyn just had to get past any fear of what his opinion of her might be.

"Well," Ren broke through Evelyn's swirling thoughts. "We have a celebration to plan."

13

The people of Heretrua celebrated like no other people. The castle ballroom was now full of food and people. It was dark outside, but the stars shone brilliantly, flowering vines covered the balcony railings, and lanterns hung from the ceiling, all setting the stage for a magical night. Lively music accompanied joyful dancing, and sounds of happiness filled the air. When Evelyn followed Jacquelyn in the door, the contagious mood made it impossible for her to feel out of place for long.

Jacquelyn led Evelyn to where Ty and Ren were waiting at the head of the room. She told Evelyn that tonight she would be playing the part of royalty. Evelyn fidgeted with her necklace. What would everyone think of her?

Ren turned to greet Evelyn and stopped to gaze at her for a moment, smiling with a fondness similar to that he showed his sister. "You look beautiful," he breathed, turning back to the crowd. As he started calling everyone to silence, Jacquelyn put her hands on her hips, and Ty winked at her. "You too, Sis." Evelyn blushed, unused to such attention.

Ren stepped forward from the other three, and the entire crowd fixed its attention on him.

"We're so glad to be celebrating this joyous occasion with all of you tonight," Ren said, his voice reaching into the far corners of the room. Evelyn smiled at how youthfulness still mingled with the commanding nature of his voice. She was glad he still had a bit of that left.

"I want to introduce you to the girl who made this celebration possible." He turned to Evelyn, took her hand, and gently pulled her forward with him. The crowd erupted into wild shouting and cheering. Evelyn smiled softly at the unrestrained welcome. She knew she didn't deserve such praise. But then again, they probably didn't know that.

Ren held up his free hand, and the room quieted again. "Evelyn came all the way from another world to win this victory for us." He turned and smiled down at her, "Thank you, Evelyn." Then softer, "Every victory counts."

Applause burst out throughout the room. Ren's hand slipped out of hers, and Evelyn was pleased to get out of the spotlight.

They should have shared the praise with her. The siblings had done far more than she ever would. Evelyn let her emotions slide slowly, savoring this beautiful moment.

Ty leapt into the dancing, Jacquelyn made her way across the room to chat, and Ren stepped back away from the noise, observing quietly. Evelyn saw the weight of an unshared burden in his face and was unsure of whether or not she should join him. After all, what help could she offer him?

Ty jumped out of the crowd behind Evelyn. She yelped in surprise. He laughed and grabbed her by the hand. "Come on, Evelyn, it's your party. Celebrate with us!" He pulled her into the dancing crowd, whirling her away into the noise.

The party lasted long into the night. The crowd never seemed to die down. Evelyn was not yet conditioned for this sort of merrymaking, so she went out on the balcony for fresh air.

She inhaled deeply. This was a breath you couldn't get in the city.

Evelyn peered back into the room, looking for Ren. What had he done with his night while she'd been dancing and celebrating like she didn't have a care in the world?

Ty appeared by her side on the balcony. "What are you thinking about?" Mischief danced in his voice. "You look as deep in thought as Ren."

Evelyn turned her head to look him in the eye. "How is

he?"

"Ren?"

Evelyn nodded. "He's disappeared on us."

"Ah." Ty shook his head. "Don't worry about him."

"Why not?

"He takes life far too seriously. He has burdens he feels are his responsibility alone, even though he has people willing to help. You can't be weighed down by that. Let me take care of him."

Evelyn gazed back out into the ball room. "He's lucky to have you."

"Believe me, I know," Ty joked. "It takes a lot of resilience to take care of Ren."

Evelyn laughed. "Where is he now then?"

"I believe he's somewhere not celebrating with us."

"There's not much for him to celebrate anyway."

Ty searched her face. "What makes you say that?"

"Well," Evelyn bit her lip. "I don't want to make assumptions."

"You don't need to worry about telling me what you think. An outside view might be refreshing about now."

Evelyn looked back to the crowd inside. Ty's gaze followed hers as she gestured towards them. "I can't imagine how I'd feel watching my people celebrate, believing they're safe and free, when I know the truth is that they're not. They all depend on you three, especially on Ren, for their very lives. If I really loved them, it would hurt not being able to truly grant them their freedom. I don't think it's that Ren doesn't want to celebrate with them. He knows he can't yet. It's a sacrifice."

Ty's smile held some admiration in it when Evelyn stopped talking, worried she was completely off track or out of bounds. "And how did you dissect my brother so fast?"

"It's just how I would feel."

Ty nodded and was quiet.

"Why can't he be healed?" Evelyn asked. She knew as well as Ren did that his leg made him a weaker link. He was frustrated beyond words at his new inability. When she was around him, she could feel the tension it created. The worst part for Evelyn was that he had lost the health of his leg for her. Now she was in the spotlight while he was off figuring out what he had to do next.

"Light cannot influence darkness, but darkness can influence light," Ty explained.

"Yes, I know that. But..." Ty held up a hand, stopping her.

"Let's just start at the beginning. You know practically nothing of Heretrua."

Evelyn leaned back against the railing and listened.

"Scaolust and Heretrua have been battling for thousands of years, so long that we don't even know why we are enemies anymore."

"I would think that eventually one of you would win."

"Well, the balance of power shifts a lot here. Heretrua started out as the stronger kingdom. That has drastically changed. This is partially because of some failed efforts on our part to fix things, the crumbling of our armies years ago, and a few advantages Scaolust has."

"What kind of failed efforts?"

"Too many to recount now. Remember, it's been thousands of years."

"Well, tell me the worst one."

The biggest failure has been repeated many times in our history, mostly before we had much knowledge of exactly how magic works. Honestly, we're still learning most of it. Rulers of the separate kingdoms have often married in an effort to bring about unity and stop the fighting, but it has always failed."

"Why?"

"Only royalty has magic, but marriage into a royal family creates magic. If you were to marry someone in any royal family anywhere around here, you would gain the type of magic they have."

"Type of magic? What do you mean by type?"

"For example, Scaolust would be dark magic. Evil. We have the opposite, light. But there are also levels of magic. Heretrua is the head kingdom of our realm, and we have the highest magic. There are kingdoms beneath us that have extremely limited or weak magic."

"So to hit it big here would be to marry you or Ren."

Ty laughed. "I've never heard it phrased that way before, but yes, I suppose you're right. Although I like to consider myself quite a catch even without my magical abilities."

Evelyn grinned. "Okay, let's see if I've got this. So, since marriage into magic creates magic, and darkness always influences the light, in marriages between light and darkness, light would always turn to dark, correct?"

Ty nodded.

"So you were always more than suspicious of Philomena."

"I knew, though I hoped it was different as much as Ren did. The difference between us was that he was willing to take the one in a million chance, which really isn't like him at all."

"So he would have married Philomena," Evelyn said matter-of-factly.

"Probably. They always do."

"And then he would have turned to darkness."

"Exactly. It's a repetitive pattern. But you saved him. You broke the cycle."

"Me? How?"

"Philomena revealed herself when you came."

Evelyn hadn't thought of that before. "Do you think she would have used Ren as a way to win ultimate power without the flower?"

"Definitely."

"Life here is pretty intense."

Ty grinned. "Yes, indeed. I love it."

"You would," Evelyn laughed. "Do all romantic relationships move to marriage so quickly around here?"

"Well, yes. Isn't that the point? Is there any other way to approach a romantic relationship?"

"Well, there's dating."

Ty looked confused.

"You've never heard of dating?"

Ty shook his head.

"I suppose that would seem odd here." Evelyn wanted to get back on topic. While she had Ty to herself she wanted as much information as possible about the land she was in. "Is there anything else I should know about Heretrua?"

Ty bit his lip, pondering, "Virgo used to be a ruler of Heretrua."

Evelyn's eyes doubled in size. Ty looked at her. "Are you that surprised after your little history lesson?"

"Well that isn't something you just casually throw out there!"

"He's also our grandfather."

Evelyn nearly fell off the balcony. "How?" she asked.

"Same as all the others."

Evelyn gave Ty a look that said she wouldn't settle for such a simple answer and he sighed dramatically.

"It went like this. Virgo was the king of Heretrua at the same time Maserta was the queen of Scaolust."

A glimmer of something that Evelyn could almost pinpoint as fear flashed through Ty's eyes. It was quickly gone, but it still worried Evelyn. Ty never appeared afraid of anything.

"Maserta was one of the most powerful rulers ever to rise to Scaolust's throne. She got Virgo to marry her, which threw the kingdom into chaos. Things went downhill fast and Heretrua was weakened. People were terrified across the realm. When someone defeats Heretrua they have already defeated the entire realm."

"You're like the gateway kingdom," Evelyn was a quick study.

"That we are. The positioning is intentional," Ty paused. "Virgo killed his own daughter and her husband, my parents, and joined Maserta. He quickly became powerful in the use of dark magic."

"Hold on a second." Evelyn was starting to trace the family lines. "If Virgo is your grandfather and Philomena is also his grandaughter..."

Ty laughed as he read her thoughts. "Philomena was Maserta's grandaughter. Not Virgo's. They were both married previously."

"Where'd Maserta go?"

"She was killed by someone else involved in dark magic. A higher member of Scaolust, her authorities."

"Why would they do something like that?"

Ty shrugged. "Beats me. She was doing a good job destroying us. Heretrua likely wouldn't still be here if Maserta had stuck around."

"Does it really matter? If light cannot influence darkness, how can Heretrua win?"

Ty smiled, and in his smile Evelyn caught sight of hope, the kind of hope that seems impossible, but never dies.

"Someday there will be one who can influence dark magic. The Queen of Light."

"But I thought you were all rulers of light."

"We rule the head of the kingdom of light, not the light itself. Technically, no one can rule over the light, but the Queen will have the highest level of magic ever. She cannot be replicated. Only she has the power to influence darkness. When this Queen comes, she will be able to conquer Scaolust. She will be able to conquer anything. Heretrua will finally have lasting peace."

"Do you know when she'll come?"

"We don't know any details, only that she will come, someday."

Evelyn stared towards Scaolust, as deep in thought as the darkness of Scaolust's inky night sky. She shuddered, suddenly cold, as if touched by a finger of evil. "I hope that day comes soon."

14

Within a few days, everything returned to normal in Heretrua. The villagers went about their daily lives, children played in the streets. Everything was peaceful. The feeling of worry was gone.

Then life shattered.

A burst of darkness exploded in the center of the village, completely disintegrating buildings, leaving some smoking as flames leaped up from the heaps of rubble. Philomena rose through the cloud of darkness, sending people fleeing for their lives or freezing them in helpless terror and despair. Philomena destroyed whatever she willed. How dare the light defy the darkness in celebration of their victory over Scaolust?

A mother managed to escape to the edge of the village. She desperately pushed her nine year old daughter up into a tree. "Climb into the thickest part," she urged. "Don't come down until I come for you. And keep quiet!"

She turned and gasped as a hand closed around her neck and shoved her back against the tree. The child screamed. Philomena smiled. "Trying to hide?"

The mother clawed at Philomena's hand, gasping for each breath.

"Now, now," Philomena crooned, leaning in closer. "Your daughter will live," she hissed. "To know what it is to long for death to take her."

Philomena's blade sunk into her victim. The world seemed silent except for the screams of one small child crying "Mommy, Mommy," over and over again.

15

Evelyn had taken it upon herself to get past Ren's exterior shell and become as close to him as she was easily growing to his siblings. She was pleased with the outcome of her efforts as they had moved past polite exchanges to friendly comfort in each other's presence.

Ren was now answering Evelyn's left over questions from her conversation with Ty while she circled the throne room, admiring the artwork on the walls and in the windows. Every piece of art sparked a new story. Heretrua's history was rich, as was Ren's personal history, or at least what snippets of it he shared.

Evelyn had grown accustomed to the distinct rhythm of Ren's footsteps now, as he followed her around the room. The cadence of his steps may have sounded strange to some, perhaps intimidating to children, but Evelyn found it musical and comfortingly familiar. She always knew when Ren was around.

"So what is it like?" Evelyn asked. "Being the top ruler?"

"That's a rather vague question."

"Well, you aren't just king of this kingdom. Heretrua is the head of all the kingdoms in the realm, isn't it?"

"Yes it is." One side of his mouth turned up. "I think about that fact far too often."

"And what is it like?"

"Stressful."

"Beyond that."

He peered at her. "It is also the most noble and rewarding task I can ever imagine performing. You never know how much you love people until you're leading them, making it your business to care and know about everything they do, until they depend on you for everything. Until their lives are in your hands." He led her to a painting on the wall. "My parents," he gestured towards the couple, "had that kind of love."

Evelyn studied his face. "So do you."

"I hope so."

Evelyn turned back to the painting. "They're so young in this picture. Is it the same with the rulers of all the kingdoms, too?"

"That's difficult to answer. I can't stereotype all the kingdoms together, but in general, each generation of rulers does seem to be younger than the last."

The two were still for a moment, looking at the painting. Evelyn wondered what it must be like to be one of the royal siblings, knowing their life would be short. And if they were to die even earlier than their parents, how would they have time to produce an heir? Would their deaths mean the end of Heretrua?

"Is it hard? Knowing the likelihood of the future?"

"You know how everyone thinks the ultimate way of showing love is to sacrifice your life for another person?"

Evelyn nodded.

"Sometimes it's even harder to keep living for them. Literally and metaphorically speaking." Ren turned to her. "Does that make sense?"

"Absolutely. It's hard to understand how dying could be a selfish thing, but in your case, I suppose it would be."

"You do understand." Ren smiled in the comfort that comes from being understood after a long time of people not understanding.

"What happens if you do die?"

Ren shrugged. "Scaolust wins."

Evelyn was about to reply when a terrible sound filled the room. She was knocked forward into the wall and then to the floor by a massive blast from the center of the room. A black mist blocked out the light.

It seemed as though the floor underneath Ren shot up. He was flipped again as another burst of black fog rolled over the room. Philomena stepped out of the fog in front of Ren.

Evelyn put a hand on her head, looking up to where Ren was rolling over on the ground. "I'm so tired of her," she muttered.

"Hello, Rennigan," Philomena said smoothly. A mass of black magic shot from her hands at Ren, who barely blocked it in time with his own magic as he edged backwards on the floor. Philomena laughed.

"You can't protect them. You aren't strong enough to keep me away." She shot two more balls of black crashing into the floor, sending Ren and Evelyn down again.

"That flower was your sole source of protection and now that it's gone? It's only a matter of time."

Evelyn started to stand. Philomena shot her to the ground again. Ren lost his focus on Philomena. For just a few seconds he wasn't looking at her. Philomena aimed to kill. Evelyn was just close enough to intervene.

Philomena unleashed magic towards Ren. Evelyn moved subconsciously, before she had time to consider any other option. She threw herself in front of Ren, knowing that was the only way they could block Philomena's magic in time.

Evelyn felt Ren throw his arms around her and a shield like the ones from the flower shot up around them. They closed their eyes and turned their heads as the black magic hit the shield and exploded outwards. A slice of amber light shot through the room, cutting through and evaporating the fog, sending Philomena away.

The shield fell down slowly and stillness settled over the room. The two young people pulled out of their defensive ball. Ren surveyed the room in disbelief and Evelyn just let herself feel safety and relief right where she was in his arms. Looking up at him, she wondered if Philomena had enjoyed her time with Ren at all. Surely she had.

"How did you do that?" Ren asked, helping her to her feet.

"I have no idea." Evelyn managed a small grin. She was shaking, quickly losing control of her body in the aftershock of the event. All at once Evelyn realized what she had done. "I was asking you the very same question not that long ago," she said. Ren caught her before she could collapse. "I feel like I just ran a marathon in the middle of a desert. Does magic do that sometimes?"

Ren took her by both shoulders and looked her in the eye. "Why did you do that? Didn't you expect to die?"

"Come on," Evelyn responded, looking up at him with eyes full of mirth already. "We just talked about this."

16

Evelyn stood silently with Jacquelyn and Ty, watching Ren survey the village. All four were in shock.

Philomena had completely destroyed most of the village. Bodies and debris were scattered all the way to the meadow. No building was left untouched. Everyone and everything was filthy. All the children were crying. Some people sat on the ground in stunned silence, some milled around surveying the damage. All were mourning.

Ren left his siblings and Evelyn without explanation. As he strode through the village, faces turned up to him. He was practically a beacon of hope walking through the village before he disappeared into one of the houses.

Ty was the only one of the three siblings who could remain optimistic in the most desperate of times. Even now he rounded up all the children and made a game of herding what animals still lived into a makeshift pen.

Evelyn was completely lost. Everywhere she looked there were helpless people, waiting for someone to help them. Admittedly, helping others was not Evelyn's strong suit.

But it had been her mother's.

Evelyn wasn't her mom. But she had watched the example in her mother her whole life, and she knew she did have something to offer. Evelyn was willing to try.

When Ren finished with his business, he had quite a surprise waiting for him. All of the unusable wood was already out of the way being burned while the wood that was in good condition was being sorted by size. The houses that had managed to stay halfway up were cleaned out, and groups of men were already putting a few back together. Any remaining food or houseware was being collected and organized for everyone to share.

Ty was still leading the kids around on the grand mission of picking up the smaller debris still scattered over the main road. Some kids had brooms, and went behind, sweeping up piles on the side of the road.

Everyone was filthy and working hard. Even Evelyn. Especially Evelyn. She was right in the thick of things, having done away with all the finery she could while remaining decent in order to work effectively. Jacquelyn was running all over the village, taking Evelyn's commands to the places they needed to go and bringing questions and requests to her.

Ren approached Evelyn as she was about to head for the bonfire, her hands full of smelly dead animals. "What's going on here?" he asked. "How did this get cleaned up so fast?"

"We're just getting a head start," Evelyn replied. "I'm not doing it wrong, am I?"

"You mean you're the one who organized all of this?"

"Yes. But I'm ready to hand things back over to you."

"No, no, don't do that! You've got this under control. Just tell me where to go and what to do." Ren bowed and Evelyn grinned.

"I'm sure you have plenty of other important things to worry about. I honestly don't have a clue what I'm doing."

"All the same." Ren straightened. "You have some amazing organizational skills."

"Thank you." Evelyn opened her mouth to say more, but stopped and cocked her head.

"What?"

Ty and the kids had continued further into the village, leaving Ren and Evelyn in the stillness of the edge.

"I thought I heard something." Evelyn shook her head. "Will you take care of those?" she asked, offering Ren handfuls of dead critters. "I don't think there is much more out here. I'll just double check before we start something else."

Ren nodded. "Sounds good," he grinned. "Who's assigning the next job, you or me?"

"It's definitely your turn." She pointed him towards the village and started to double check the area one last time.

Everything seemed taken care of until Evelyn turned back towards the village. She gasped and dropped everything. "Ren!" she screamed. "Come here!" She saw him look back at her. "Hurry!" she pleaded.

Ren started running and Evelyn stepped off the road tentatively, one slow step at a time until she was close enough to see the whole horrid scene.

"Oh no." She sank to her knees and forced herself to examine the little girl crumpled on the ground next to her dead mother. The girl was gasping for each breath, sweating and shaking violently. Leaning farther over, Evelyn found that the girl had a death grip on a dagger plunged deep into her side.

Ren was by Evelyn's side in an instant. "She's still alive?"

Evelyn felt dizzy. The girl's eyes were locked onto hers and no matter how hard she tried, Evelyn could not break eye contact with the child.

"This is too far," Ren's face turned to stone. "Stay with her. I'm getting help." As he stood, Evelyn latched onto his arm. She looked up at him, desperation in her eyes. "Please hurry," she whispered. Ren nodded and she let him go.

Evelyn and the child stared at each other for a long time, both in different stages of shock. The girl's breathing made Evelyn's stomach roll. She felt completely helpless. Watching the child's agony while waiting for Ren was driving her mad.

Evelyn took the girl's free hand in her own. Instantly, the child had a vice-like grip. Evelyn winced.

"You'll be safe soon," Evelyn promised, though she didn't know if it was true. She looked back at the dagger. "You have to let go of that okay? That way when Ren comes back we can get it out." Talking out loud wasn't getting any response out of the girl, but it was helping Evelyn all the same. "I'm going to help you let go, alright?"

Evelyn leaned over and placed her hand over the little girl's. One by one, she pried off the paralyzed fingers and covered both of the girl's hands with her own.

Evelyn took a deep, shuddering breath. Surprisingly, her ability to deal with the situation thrown at her was improving minute by minute. "We have help coming," she assured the girl, squeezing her hands.

Finally, Ren, Ty, and a doctor showed up. They all knelt around the child as the doctor got right to work. His movements were swift and expert. Evelyn could see the girl's eyes moving the slightest bit, watching his every move. The doctor looked the girl in the eye and said, "You won't want to watch this, sweetie."

Ren met Evelyn's eyes from the other side of the child and she bit her lip. "Just look at me," Evelyn prompted.

The child complied. Evelyn smiled at her. "That's right. You'll be okay." Evelyn was glad not to watch either as the doctor pulled out the dagger. The child gasped and shuddered, grasping Evelyn's arm like a lifeline before going limp.

The next thing Evelyn knew, Ty was leading her away from the scene, thrusting her bloody hands into a cold stream.

"Evelyn, you have to get a grip. The doctor will take care of her."

Evelyn tried to swallow her tears. "She's so little, she's so young." She shook her head and swiped at her eyes viciously. "Will she live?"

"I don't know," Ty responded.

"But you have magic, can't you use that to help her?"

"To a certain extent."

Evelyn buried her face in her hands. Ty pulled her hands away and forced her to look him in the eye. "Evelyn. We're fighting in a never ending battle. It's brutal, too much blood and too many tears. People die. I hate it too, but you have to be prepared to deal with the pain. Sitting here crying won't help that little girl." He gestured out towards the village. "It's not helping any of them. You can't just feel bad." He took Evelyn's hand firmly. "To make a difference, you have to keep yourself together and go do something about it."

17

At the end of the day everyone gathered to eat and comfort one another around bonfires. If trouble wasn't looming overhead and sorrow and grief looming in their hearts it would have been a lovely time.

Evelyn sat with a large family whose father had died. The mother nursed her baby and gazed into space in mournful silence while Evelyn fed the toddler and tried to comfort the oldest daughter. Not only was it difficult to find words, but Evelyn's own heart was heavy. She watched the door of the makeshift hospital attentively.

Everyone would sleep with a roof over their head that night, even if it was a bit crowded. Ren consulted with Ty, and they decided they would stay in the village that night to keep everything in order and just in case Philomena decided to come back. Ren tried to send Evelyn back to the castle, but she had other ideas.

"Is Jacquelyn staying here?" Evelyn asked.

"Yes," Ren admitted.

"If Jacquelyn's staying, I'm staying," she declared.

Ren looked over her head to Ty for help. Ty just shrugged. Ren sighed, and Evelyn put her hands on her hips. "I'm not leaving. Especially not alone and not while I can still be useful here."

"Fine. Just please, stay safe. You never know what's going to happen out here."

"Or anywhere in Heretrua." Evelyn was recovering a bit of her spiritedness. "Are you forgetting who saved you from Philomena? Twice? I'll be fine."

She set off to find Jacquelyn. Ty grinned at his brother. "A girl without magic or knowledge of our ways is making a habit of saving you?"

Ren shoved his brother good naturedly as he walked by. "I can take care of myself. She's just quicker than me."

Evelyn and Jacquelyn stayed together in the hospital. Jacquelyn was naturally gifted at tending to the sick, and Evelyn, though not gifted, wanted to stay close to the little girl she had found by the road. Ren and Ty stayed with the villagers in the other four buildings, alternating buildings every few hours, generally keeping an eye on things.

The night was stormy. Rain poured from the sky like a waterfall. When the wind picked up there was whimpering from the children and worried whispering from the mothers. The storm continued to build and fear mounted along with it.

The door flew open and the wind blew out all the lanterns. A chorus of screams rose. Jacquelyn's magic glowed purple in her hands, lighting the room once again, and everyone settled down.

"Why don't you do that all the time?" Evelyn asked as she closed the door and knelt on the ground next to Jacquelyn.

"Magic wears us out the way normal work does," Jacquelyn explained. "When we get too tired, our magic is also weaker. We only use it when absolutely necessary."

A shriek came from one of the mothers. It was different than the other frightened cries. Jacquelyn ran to the back of the room. She returned to Evelyn with news that one of the kids was missing. A quick search of the building revealed he wasn't inside. Jacquelyn burst out the door. Evelyn dropped her blankets to rush after her.

They were both stunned by the water. Raindrops stung Evelyn's cheeks. The girls were drenched at once. No one would have guessed that a road was once in the place of this river rushing through the village.

Jacquelyn made her magic shine brighter, lighting the

path the water was taking. "No child could handle something like this," she yelled over the noise of the wind.

"We have to find him anyway," Evelyn urged. "Keep the light on for me." She stepped into the water and was instantly pulled under. Her hands caught hold of a tree's roots and she pulled herself back up, gasping and coughing.

Evelyn surveyed the river ahead of her. Jacquelyn's light still guided her, but dimly. "I need more light!" she called. Then she spotted something. "I think I see him!"

Jacquelyn directed her light to where Evelyn was pointing. "How are you going to get to him?"

Evelyn reached for another hold, grabbed it, and pulled herself forward.

"Be careful!" Jacquelyn warned.

Evelyn ran out of places to grab and looked up again. A tree had been knocked down into the water and a small boy was caught in the branches. He was struggling to stay above the water. The branches prevented him from being swept farther down, but they also kept him from pulling himself farther up.

Evelyn had to get to him. She let go of her hold and heard Jacquelyn scream as she was swept down again. When her head broke the surface, Evelyn could hear Jacquelyn calling to her, then the light vanished as she ran for help.

"Jacquelyn, come back! I need the-" Evelyn was cut off as water swept over her once more.

18

Evelyn made it to the boy's tree and clung to its branches desperately. She had to get down to where the boy was. The water washed over her head again and again. She couldn't see much.

Finally Evelyn reached the exhausted boy. She wedged herself between the branches, then reached out for the boy. Pulling him to her, she held him tight above the water.

The boy wrapped his arms around her neck and buried his face in her shoulder. Evelyn held him and sighed, grateful to catch her breath. She was perfectly willing to wait here for a minute until she had a plan. It was safer than trying to move.

Another wave hit, and she was knocked loose. Evelyn grabbed desperately at a branch and pulled herself and the boy above the water as he whimpered and clung tighter.

Evelyn could do nothing but hold on as water continued to wash over them. Her arms started to ache. Keeping the child in her arms and both of them above water was really impossible. Everything worked against them. The water, the wind, the branches creaking underneath them.

Out of the darkness, strong arms reached around Evelyn and the boy, pulling them both safely away from the water and up onto the trunk of the huge tree. They lifted the burden from Evelyn and wrapped around her shoulders. Light flooded the area from the person's hand, revealing Ren's face.

"Evelyn."

"I'm sorry."

"I told you to stay safe."

"I tried."

Ren held the child and he and Evelyn helped each other along, Ren's limp heavy, Evelyn shivering, all three chilled to the bones. The trek back to the village was slow.

An overjoyed mother greeted them at the door of the building, making the struggle worth it as she took her child from Ren's arms.

Ren handed Evelyn off to Jacquelyn and collapsed on the floor. Jacquelyn wrapped Evelyn in blankets and made her lay down next to the injured girl. Evelyn looked at Ren and he smiled at her.

"It's a good thing I let you stay after all," he said.

Evelyn returned his smile. "Like you had a choice." She rolled over to sleep, but the little girl was awake, staring at her.

"I want to be just like you and save people," she whispered.

Satisfied, Evelyn squeezed the girl's hand and let herself fall into a deep sleep.

It was obvious now that Scaolust was still a threat, that Heretrua was still in constant danger. That fact was impossible to ignore. Scaolust could strike again at any time. Ren sent Ty to retrieve some soldiers to protect the village, then explained to the villagers that it was unlikely Scaolust would strike here again. Scaolust wanted the rulers, not the people.

Evelyn was in great danger, too, as she was in close contact with all three rulers at all times. Ren couldn't tell if Evelyn realized the danger for herself or not. She was very aware of the danger for Heretrua royalty, so she had to understand how she was affected by that. What should they do with her? Let her fight alongside them or send her away? Ren didn't want to let her know that there was little chance any of them would avoid death and defeat for long.

19

Even after the siblings and Evelyn returned to the castle, things were far from back to normal. Everything was uncertain. Philomena's display of power was unnerving. What more could Virgo be capable of?

"What exactly does Scaolust want?" Evelyn asked from her seat on the floor.

"We really have no idea," Ren told her. "They're just determined to destroy us for no apparent reason other than a lust for power."

"What do you plan to do now?"

"I don't know."

"They want us," Jacquelyn said. "As long as we survive, they shouldn't bother the people too much."

"But they already did." Evelyn looked to each of the siblings. "Why did they do that?"

Ty looked at Ren and the brothers shared a silent exchange before Ty said, "That was an individual act of Philomena for fun. She's just that cruel."

Ren turned away from his brother. Evelyn could see irritation in his eyes.

Ty continued, "If I could just kill her, forget about Virgo, this whole battle would be a lot more straightforward."

"Ty..." Ren countered.

"Oh, you don't want me to kill her?" Ty raised an eyebrow. "You want me to settle down? This is war, Ren. Sooner or later, one of us is going to have to do it."

Ren leaned against a wall and glared at Ty without saying a word.

"We should probably get Evelyn one of these," Ty changed the subject, slapping the arm of his throne. "So she doesn't have to sit on the floor anymore."

"She does deserve one." Ren smiled and directed the rest of his words towards Evelyn. "Since you've saved us on numerous occasions."

"I like the floor just fine," Evelyn said. "I'm certainly not royalty."

"Not yet," Ty corrected, catching a surprised glance from his siblings. "What?"

"You ought to be," Ren said, moving away from the wall and venturing towards the condensed group. "You handle yourself like you are."

"Well, I'm pleased to be able to serve here, and I'm grateful you've all accepted me."

"I'm glad you like it here," Ren said. "Heretrua is a very dangerous place to live right now."

"It's dangerous where I live, too," Evelyn told him. "Maybe not as dangerous, but it could be. It's worth it here."

"Good," Ty said. "Because it looks like you're stuck with us."

"Even if I wasn't stuck," Evelyn said, looking up at Ren as she spoke. "At this point I wouldn't choose to leave."

Ren helped her up and offered his arm to Evelyn. "Come on. Let's go see your little friend."

The little girl found with a dagger in her side had been moved, upon Evelyn's request, into the castle. Evelyn hadn't yet been able to discuss with Ren why she felt it was so important to have nine year old Genneviera under such close supervision, but Ren had easily agreed with her, thus no explanation was needed.

"Other than her mother, Genneviera has no family to speak of," Ren informed Evelyn as they walked down the halls. "She has no place to live and no one to take care of her."

"In that case, can I keep her?"

Ren cocked an eyebrow. "Keep her?"

"She could be my personal companion. It would be fun to have a little girl around." Evelyn grinned, bittersweet. "We're really in the same boat, Genne and I."

"Well then, if she accepts it, we've got a plan." Ren pushed the door open for Evelyn. She went in quietly and sat on the edge of Genne's bed. The girl's eyes were barely open, but she was awake.

"Hey, Genne," Evelyn said softly. "How are you doing?"

The girl's mouth hardly moved when she talked, and her voice was terribly quiet. "Are you the one who saved me?"

Evelyn was about to deny that she had done anything, but Ren stepped up behind her. "Yes," he said. "She's the one."

"You saved a little boy, too," Genne continued. "Will I be able to do that someday?"

"You can do anything you set your mind to," Evelyn told her. "Can you do me a favor and set your mind to getting better?"

The girl nodded. "What will happen to me then?"

"Well," Evelyn looked up at Ren, a question in her eyes.

"That depends," he said. "If you would enjoy it, you can live here in the castle as one of Evelyn's personal maids. Otherwise, we'll have to think of a new plan."

Genne's eyes brightened. "I can live in the castle with her?"

"If you're sure that's what you want."

"Oh, yes, thank you!" Her whispered gratitude was endearing.

"Good. I'm excited to get to know you, Genne," Evelyn said. "I'm sure we'll become good friends." The woman tending to Genne shot a warning look in their direction. Evelyn heeded her warning. "I think we need to let you rest now. Work on feeling better for me fast, okay?"

"Okay." Genne smiled and closed her eyes. Ren and Evelyn left.

"Well," Ren closed the door softly and turned to Evelyn. "I think she's going to be just fine."

Evelyn sighed. "That's a relief. Thank you, Ren."

20

Awakened by the morning light, Evelyn was struck by a sharp pang of loneliness. She wanted company. She swung her legs out of bed and stumbled over to the bell rope in the corner.

Her maids were already in the sitting room when Evelyn got there. She had never been around a more eager, cheerful, and efficient group of ladies, though Evelyn was still getting used to being waited on all the time.

"Could someone please get me breakfast?" Evelyn asked. "And the rest of you... I'm sorry, but I'm still not able to get these clothes to work correctly on my own."

"That's what we're here for," offered one young girl as she cheerfully dove into the closet to pick Eveyln's dress. Genneviera followed close on her heels and Evelyn smiled. Genne had healed quickly with the astute care in the castle. She was an eager learner and her smiles and energy never failed to make Evelyn's day.

"What are you doing today, Evelyn?" Genne called from inside the closet.

"Oh, I don't know." Evelyn was having a bout of homesickness. She really needed some sort of stability to lean on. "I think if Ren isn't busy I'd like to talk to him about a few things." She turned to the adults. "Do you know Ren's schedule for the day?"

"Ah, the king," Genneviera cooed. There were muffled giggles and chatter from inside the closet. Evelyn raised a questioning eyebrow at the other ladies, who just chuckled and shook their heads.

"In that case, you're going to need something fancier than this," Genne called out brightly.

"And something special for her hair!" The other girl

chimed in and they started babbling back and forth.

Evelyn peeked into the closet. "Girls, I see Ren all the time. You don't need to dress me up for him."

"Why not?" The girls responded in unison. Genne beckoned to another servant. "Go tell the king to come fetch Evelyn in about an hour," she commanded importantly.

The woman winked at Evelyn. "You won't be bothering him," she assured her before disappearing through the door.

Another lady started unlacing Evelyn's night gown.

"Do you think she's right?" Evelyn asked her.

"About what?"

"About me not bothering him? I'm sure he's got better things to do. I've been enough of a distraction already."

"Sweetie, Ren needs a distraction."

Evelyn was quiet and the woman came around front to look her in the face. Her smile was comforting, motherly. "You are in need of one, too, aren't you?"

Evelyn nodded.

Ren arrived just as Evelyn was standing from breakfast.

"Hello, ladies," he nodded to the servants as he strode towards Evelyn. "What did you need me for?"

"Um," Evelyn decided to simply admit the truth. "Loneliness."

"Ah." His eyes softened as he stepped back. "Come on."

He led her to the hallway. "We've never given you an official tour of the castle, have we? Would you like to have one today?"

"That would be fun."

"Good. Then we'll start outside and work our way in. But I don't want to ruin the surprises of any parts you haven't seen by walking through them on our way." Ren grinned, and snapped his fingers. All at once they were at the gate to the gardens. "Perfect!"

Evelyn was starting to get used to people around her using magic, but she still knew it was an honor to have it used on her the way it was.

Ren lead Evelyn forward into a magnificent garden like none other she had ever seen. It was like a maze, complete with streams, bridges, trees, shrubs, more colors than Evelyn knew could exist, fountains, benches, and unidentifiable fruits. A surprise could be found behind every corner. It was wonderful.

"There are some amazing things out here," Ren said. "Ask me any question you can think of and I'll find a gardener to help us answer them."

"How great is the threat from Scaolust? Really?" Evelyn surprised herself with this question.

"Oh... I don't think the gardeners will have the answer to that one." Ren took the question in stride and held out his hand to help Evelyn up some steep steps. "Before you picked the flower we had some protection. Yet we still feared for our lives because Scaolust is talented at finding a way around every defense. Now that our protection is gone, the threat is even larger than before."

"That's what I was thinking. Rather than making things better for you, my coming here has made things worse."

Ren sighed. "That's not totally accurate."

"Don't lie to me."

"Define 'lie.'"

"Ren. If I didn't want to know, I wouldn't ask."

There was silence for a moment as they walked along, Ren staring at the ground. "Honestly, Evelyn, we're doomed. There's no hope left, nothing to find encouragement in. Now that our protection is gone, it's only a matter of time. We can try to defend ourselves, but the darkness is so much more powerful than us." He looked up at her. "But that doesn't make it your fault. Time was running out either way."

"What is Scaolust waiting for then?"

He shook his head. "Nothing. They're just cruel. Like a cat with a mouse."

Evelyn caught a glimpse of some squirrels chasing each other. Good. She would have missed squirrels if Heretrua didn't have them.

"Ty still seems to have hope."

"He'll carry that with him to the grave."

"You say that like it's a bad thing."

"I don't see the point in putting my trust in something not there to see."

"Which is what, exactly?"

Ren sighed. "Ty is waiting, as all the realm is waiting, for the Queen of Light. I don't really believe in a Queen of Light anymore. If I did, I don't know when, where, or how she could come to us."

"Isn't there proof though?"

"Oh there are plenty of legends."

"Why does Ty believe in them and you don't?"

"Where would she come from, Evelyn? Legends come from people's wishes, what they want to be true. No one can influence darkness."

"Why not?"

"I don't know. It doesn't need to be understood."

"Anything the majority of the people believe in should be understood, especially by their leaders."

Ren smiled. "Well then, it's a good thing I have Ty around."

"So the honest answer is we are completely powerless against Scaolust."

Ren shrugged apologetically. "You wanted the truth."

"How do you keep acting so optimistic?"

"It's my job. Being king isn't about how I feel."

Evelyn desperately wanted Ren to be wrong about the Queen of Light. After all, no one could know everything all the time.

The two continued their conversation, switching between serious topics and just enjoying friendly banter. It was one of the few easy, enjoyable thing they could do.

Ren's position was a unique one. He was one of the youngest kings in the history of Heretrua, yet he already had more power than most of the other kings had when they were at their highest point of glory. Knowing that gave Evelyn a small glimpse of how much magic the kingdoms were dealing with right now. Scaolust must have massively powerful magic too, to be setting these royal siblings back so much.

All at once, an indescribably awful sound, a screech crossed with a roar, shook the castle's foundations. It was the kind of sound that set Heretrua apart with all certainty as a whole different world than Evelyn's home.

The floor trembled beneath them. Evelyn looked at Ren when the sound stopped. "What was that?"

21

The sound bellowed through the walls again. Evelyn followed Ren as he hurried through the castle.

Jacquelyn joined them. "What's going on?" she gasped.

"I have no idea," Evelyn replied as another roar pierced the air. "I was going to ask you the same thing." A series of short screeches followed. Ty ran between the two girls and up the hallway, obviously excited by the sounds.

"Let's go find out!" he called.

Evelyn and Jacquelyn followed, feeling much safer with the boys than without them, even if they were moving closer to the noise instead of away from it.

Ty led them outside where Ren was already peering off towards Scaolust. All four knew that was where it had to be coming from.

"I've never heard anything like this before," Ren said. "Do you have any idea what it is, Ty?"

The prince shook his head, grinning. "I have no idea."

"Ty, this is not a good thing," Evelyn chided.

All at once, something shot up straight towards the sky from the waters behind the Scaolust castle. Lunging over the dark castle, the creature landed on the meadow in front of it. It let out another screeching roar and all four people in Heretrua took a step backwards.

"That's big," Ren whispered.

"It's a...snake?" Evelyn guessed weakly.

"It's a dragon," Jacquelyn said with certainty.

"It's a sea serpent," Ty admired the creature.

"I don't even want to find out," Ren said.

As if in response, the creature started moving towards Heretrua.

"What are we going to do about it?" Jacquelyn was

starting to panic.

"We need to slow it down first," Ty said, always the one formulating a plan.

"Then what?"

"We'll cross that bridge when we get to it." Ty held open his hands, filling them with blue magic. Ren nodded in agreement and brought magic to his hands too. Together they threw their magic into the air. It formed a swirling ball above their heads.

Evelyn stepped back and watched, feeling helpless and yet astonished by the talent of these siblings. They seemed able to read each others minds, their movements were flawlessly synchronized.

They let loose their magic and it flew out towards the creature. Bursting in its face, the magic formed a wall to block the creature from getting any closer to Heretrua. It bellowed and rammed its head into the wall to break through.

"It'll get through soon," Ren said.

"Now what?" Jacquelyn asked.

Ty looked at his brother first for confirmation, then stared back out at the creature they were facing. "We can't let it come here. We're going to have to go to it."

"What?" Jacquelyn cried. "I thought we were trying to stay away from it!"

"No," Ty said. "We're trying to kill it."

"How do you plan to do that?"

"I don't know yet, but I doubt you've got a better solution."

"Come on, Jacquelyn," Ren said. "We have to get rid of that thing."

The creature was determined. There was limited time. Evelyn would have to watch in agony.

22

From Evelyn's view, the humans looked like insects compared to the creature. Ty managed to slip behind it, unnoticed until he struck it from behind.

This did nothing but make the monster mad. It screamed, flinging itself down at Ty. The prince threw a bubble of protection around himself. The beast smashed down on it, yet Ty remained unhurt.

The creature reared up in preparation to smash once more, but this time Ren hit him. The creature turned on Ren, who ran to the forest where Jacquelyn was waiting.

The monster drew itself up to an enormous height and crashed down onto the forest.

That hadn't been expected. Evelyn held her breath as trees snapped like toothpicks. The beast drew back, looking for its prey. Evelyn couldn't see Ren or Jacquelyn.

Ty directed his magic into a ball above the creature's head. It twisted to hiss at him. White and purple light joined Ty's in the air. Evelyn breathed a sigh of relief. Ren and Jacquelyn were unharmed.

The siblings dropped their magic onto the beast's head. The explosion temporarily blocked Evelyn's view.

Yet again, the creature rose, undefeated. Enraged, it lashed out furiously at the two in the forest headfirst while lashing at Ty with its tail. It missed Ren and Jacquelyn, but Ty was thrown down hard. Luckily, the creature wasn't interested in him right now. It struck again at the other two, who managed to deter it, but just barely.

Ty got up. The beast didn't notice him climbing up its back, it was so intently focused on his siblings. Ty got close to its head, then struck hard with his magic, piercing its flesh, aiming for the heart.

He apparently struck close to home. The serpent rose up and roared, almost deafening them all. Ty held on for dear life. Ren leaped into the air, using his magic to join Ty. What they could do with their magic never ceased to surprise Evelyn.

The brothers took aim and struck together. Jacquelyn added her magic from the ground. All three hit at the same time.

They struck home. The serpent screeched long, piercing the air for miles. Evelyn covered her ears and watched it fall. Jacquelyn dashed to get out of harm's way as Ren and Ty struck again. It took several blows, each one bringing another terrible cry from the creature, until at last it was still.

23

Evelyn met the siblings at the castle doors. Immediately, Ren released Jacquelyn into Evelyn's arms. The girl sobbed into Evelyn's shoulder as she held her. "I can't do this anymore."

Evelyn looked at Ren for an explanation of Jacquelyn's breakdown, but Ty interrupted as his brother opened his mouth.

"Before you all get gloomy, I want to remind everyone that this is not that big of a deal. We took care of it just fine, didn't we?"

"That's only the beginning, Ty," Ren said, frustrated. "You know they're just taunting us."

"And?"

"So maybe it's not that big of a deal compared to what we've got coming. But if this shakes us up so much, how can we stand a chance against all of Scaolust's power at once?"

"I'm not shaken up."

"That's because you're a fool." Ren turned to walk away but Ty caught him by the shoulder, throwing him back around to face him.

"I'd rather be a fool and go down fighting than be cowardly like you."

"I am fighting!"

"But you've already given up!"

"I'm just being realistic."

"Well then knock it off."

Evelyn stepped between them. "You're both acting like children. You're not going to get anything done while you're fighting with each other."

Ren looked at her, startled at her boldness. "I'm not the one believing in fairy tales."

"Maybe it's okay to give stories a chance now and then."

"Oh, is that what you believe?"

"Is that wrong?" Ty asked.

"It is if it's doing this to people," Ren gestured to Jacquelyn, who was settled down enough to be watching the argument. She opened her mouth to speak, looking indignant, but Ty cut her off.

"Your beliefs are doing this! Hope keeps people alive. Your realism makes life look hopeless and meaningless."

Jacquelyn let out a little growl of frustration. "I am perfectly capable of dealing with my own emotions, and neither of your opinions are singlehandedly making me a mess. I just deal with stress differently than you. Maybe you should let me deal with it in my own way instead of making it worse by colliding so fiercely!"

The brothers were silenced by Jacquelyn's outburst. Evelyn pulled her back gently and led her away from the scene.

The boys stood in furious silence for a moment. Ren turned to Ty again and fought to keep his voice calm and low. "Whatever your opinion is, it's not worth us arguing in front of other people. You can trust that I'll do what is in the best interest of the people. And you would do well to remember that I'm the king here. Not you."

Ren walked away and Ty fought the urge to yell at his retreating back. It wasn't worth it. He had other matters that needed tended to.

24

Evelyn sat uncomfortably, watching Jacquelyn storm about her rooms.

"Why do they have to disagree? Why can't I just agree with one opinion?"

"You agree with both of them?"

"Yes!" Jacquelyn threw her hands in the air. "So why can't they see each other's perspectives?"

"What do you agree with each of them about?"

Jacquelyn resumed her rampage. "I know Ty's right, that we need to have hope, we have to keep going. And I do believe in the Queen of Light."

"And Ren really doesn't?"

Jacquelyn shook her head. "I do think it's likely her coming is far beyond our lifetime. Which leads to where I agree with Ren. If she doesn't come now, how can we possibly win this? Where will the next generation come from?"

"Jacquelyn, those are entirely opposite ideas."

"But do they have to be?"

"Yes!"

"Ugh, I know that!" Jacquelyn plopped down on the floor, exhausted. "But they're both my brothers. They're both wise."

"Who do you really believe?" Evelyn dropped to the floor across from Jacquelyn.

"Neither," the princess admitted. "I know that sounds silly."

Evelyn shook her head. "No, it's not. That way you don't have to pick a side."

"Reality just seems too harsh to be true, and on the other side, what we hope for seems too perfect to be true. I can't give up hope. I have to believe, however unrealistic, because..." Jacquelyn met Evelyn's gaze. "What could be true is too horrible to bear."

"Then keep believing." Evelyn took Jacquelyn's hands in her own. "That's what I think Ren needs, whether he agrees with you or not."

"All the evidence we have for hope is in legends."

"No, you don't have to believe in a Queen of Light, or any other legend. You have to have Ty's hope, and you have to place it in Ren. Isn't that why he keeps going, despite his beliefs? Because of all the hope placed in him?"

"Whose side are you on?"

Evelyn laughed. "The same side we're all on. Ren's side."

"Even Ty?"

"You know he is. More than both of us combined."

"It's sad." Jacquelyn leaned her forehead on her hand. "Ren's the only one not on his own side."

Ty entered the room at that moment, opening the door a bit too roughly. Frustration was still on his face, though he was making an effort to control it.

"I wanted to apologize to both of you," he said. "Ren and I should learn to control ourselves. We're both tense, and we both acted foolishly." He looked at Evelyn. "This isn't how things usually are."

"It isn't?" Jacquelyn cocked an eyebrow.

Ty sighed. "We're in desperate times. None of us are at our best."

"You don't have to concern yourself about me," Evelyn said. "If I slow things down or complicate matters..."

Ty waved the thought off with his hand. "You're no bother, Evelyn."

"I'm certainly no help, either."

"Evelyn, you're practically family," Jacquelyn insisted.

"That doesn't make me useful." She looked at Ty. "We're going into a war, are we not?"

Ty nodded.

"I have no knowledge, tactics, skills, magic, no way to contribute to a battle, let alone any way to defend myself."

"We don't expect you to," Jacquelyn started.

"But we could."

The girls looked up at Ty, curious. He smiled mischievously. "I can teach you how to make a contribution."

Jacquelyn rolled her eyes. "Oh, brother."

"No, I'm serious."

"Believe me, I know you are."

"What are you going to do?" Evelyn asked.

Ty exchanged a glance with Jacquelyn, then smiled and beckoned the girls to follow him. "We'll show you."

25

It seemed to Evelyn that Ty was far too excited, considering the area of the castle he was showing her was full of tools of war. Tools designed to help people kill other people more effectively.

"I'm not so sure I want my contribution to look like this, Ty," she called forward to him.

"Doesn't matter," he yelled back. "I'm not going to be your personal body guard."

He disappeared and Jacquelyn joined Evelyn.

"I do this training, too," she said. "It's not that bad. We have a lot of fun here."

"How can wielding deadly objects against other human beings with the intent to kill them be considered 'fun?'"

"This isn't war."

"Yes it is." Ty was back.

"Anyway, it isn't war against people. Not here. This is me perfecting the ability to defend myself, and Ty showing off."

Ty handed Jacquelyn a bow and arrow. "When I'm done with you, you'll be able to do both." He nodded towards a target across the room. "Show her what you've got."

Jacquelyn proceeded to shoot one arrow after another with impressive speed and accuracy. As she went, Ty nudged Evelyn. "Not as bad as you thought?"

"Like Jacquelyn said, this isn't war."

"You'll be fine. I don't expect you to become a soldier." Ty nodded Jacquelyn over. "Wanna teach Evelyn how to use that or show her your hand to hand skills?"

Jacquelyn handed Evelyn the bow. "Still working on hand to hand combat."

Ty grinned. "Then I'll show her." He ran off like an excited child.

Evelyn shoved the bow back into Jacquelyn's hands. "I am not ready for this."

"It's fine not to be ready, but you have to do it anyway. You won't ever be ready. We don't get a lot of time to prepare or plan, we just get attacked and defend ourselves, which is exactly why we do this training."

Ty re-entered the room, surrounded by a group of strong men, all carrying some type of weapon. Ty talked and laughed with them as easily as if he was one of them. He fit right in. More than that, he was their leader.

The group moved to the center of the room, a wide open area, and the men formed a circle around Ty, who motioned to Evelyn. "Come close enough to watch," he called.

The men glanced at Evelyn and laughed at the prince. "Showing off, Ty?"

"Isn't that what training is for?" He got into position. "Ready?"

His men followed suit. Evelyn realized Ty was going to take them all on at once. Before she had time to be surprised or make a comment, the fight had begun.

Evelyn stepped back again to avoid the clamor. She peeked at Jacquelyn, and found the princess laughing. She had seen her brother do this before.

By the time Ty had finished and the entire group was surrendering to him in true, good-natured defeat, Evelyn was sitting with Jacquelyn, at this point every bit as amused as everyone else, though far more impressed.

Ty approached the girls, glowing with exertion and pride. He pointed at Evelyn. "That's how you're going to fight when I'm done with you."

26

Ty entered the library cautiously. Rather than finding Ren still in his rage, Ty found him sitting at a table cluttered with books and papers with his head in his hands. He looked exhausted.

When he heard Ty approaching, Ren lifted his head and swiveled hastily. He gestured towards the messy table. "I can't find anything hopeful. Not in history, not in legends, not in battle schemes or techniques. I'm out of ideas. I need more options."

"I'm sure you'll be fine, you're just worn out."

"No, we won't be fine. There's nothing."

Ty leaned over the table and pushed a few papers around to look at Ren's research. "You've got all the research and material we need."

Ren slapped his hand down over the papers. "On this table, yes. In numbers and power, no way."

"Well, at least we've got a start."

"We?" Ren shook his head. "You don't even agree with me. And a start is all we'll ever have." He turned back to the shelves and started searching through the books. Ty started sifting through the material on the table.

"I don't have to agree with you."

"Don't kid yourself. We've been arguing far too often lately."

"We're brothers. Of course we're going to argue." Ty lifted the stack of books he had deemed useless off the table. "But you're my king as much as you are my brother. I'm here to help you. I know my place, and it is not to take command."

Ren turned back to the table. Ty looked at his new books, shook his head, and took those from his hands too."Ren, I support you. And, believe it or not," Ty sat down. "I do agree with you."

Ren gave Ty a look.

"Maybe not a hundred percent. But on what is important, we do agree. Queen of Light or not, this is war, and we are the leaders. We cannot wait for someone else to do our job. We have to defend our people." Ty put a finger on one of Ren's sketches. "And we both know that I'm the war expert here."

"Are you willing to help me without asking me to wait for a miracle?"

"If that is what you need me to do."

"It is. I need something real, something tested and proven to be effective."

"Fine. But you have to give me something in return."

Ren narrowed his eyes. Ty grinned.

"You have to have hope. You have to at least try to believe we can do this."

Ren sighed. "The facts are all lined up against us. The numbers, the power."

"Ah, but the genius. That lies up here." Ty tapped on his head. "They don't have that, do they? And they also don't have trust or teamwork. We've held this thing together for a long time. Don't give up on me now."

Ren bit his lip, pondering. "Do you really believe that with the right plan, we can make this work?"

"Absolutely. If you want it badly enough."

Ren smiled. "You're such a fool," he said, this time affectionately.

"Let's be fools together, shall we?"

27

Amused, Jacquelyn watched from the side as Ty marched in front of Evelyn importantly.

"The goal of this training is self-defense. We first must find you a suitable weapon and then teach you how not to kill yourself with it." He stopped moving and looked at Evelyn for emphasis. "That would defeat the purpose of self-defense."

Evelyn suppressed a giggle and played along as seriously as Ty. She nodded solemnly. "Of course."

"Good." He motioned to her. "Stand up."

Evelyn obeyed and Ty circled her with drama. "You're pretty small, even for a girl."

"Hey, I'm not that small."

Ty raised his eyebrows.

Evelyn wasn't about to be pushed any lower than she had to be. "It doesn't matter that much, does it?"

Evelyn didn't like the look of Ty's smile after she said that. He held out his sword to her. "Hold this."

As soon as Ty let go, Evelyn's arm dropped and she grabbed with both hands to keep from dropping it on her feet.

"Wow, that is heavy!" She handed it back to Ty, jealous of how easily he handled it.

"You've never held a sword before?"

"No."

"What kind of world are you from?"

Evelyn just shrugged. She supposed it was no use protesting about how easy it seemed to use swords in movies. Ty moved on anyway.

"For now, let's stick with something appropriate for you in your current state."

"Which is?"

"Small and out of shape."

Evelyn looked at Jacquelyn in exasperation and the princess laughed at her.

"If you can't use your weapon right away, it will be useless." Ty made a good point.

He found a pair of daggers and showed them to Evelyn. "These will be fun to start with," he said, a twinkle in his eye. His almost childlike excitement was starting to rub off on Evelyn. Curiosity and a desire to learn was growing inside of her against her will.

"Two?"

"Of course!" He handed them to her.

"Ah, yes, these are easier already."

"I do have to warn you, it's going to seem like we do a lot of boring, unimportant stuff first, but it's all important. You know me, I won't do anything boring unless it's really important."

"True."

Ty grinned. "We'll be down here often to practice. You'll move on to more exciting exercises soon enough. In the end, your weapon should feel like a part of you. Think of it as an extension of your body."

"How quickly do you think I can learn?"

"Generally, I wouldn't be able to get you where I want you to be in the time frame we have, but we have to try. Nothing I can do will be of any use if you don't want it yourself. You have to own this, put a lot of time and your full effort into it. If you want to live, that is. The direction things are taking right now, you need to be able to put up a good defense without even thinking about it."

Jacquelyn stepped in. "Because as much as we want to protect you, Evelyn, we can't. We have our own battles to fight. We're key targets, which means we may not even make it through ourselves. Honestly-" She looked at Ty, who made direct eye contact with Evelyn.

"You're a key target, too."

28

    When Evelyn's first training session was over, she followed Ty to a back room, another issue pressing at the back of her mind. He didn't realize she was there until he turned around and almost ran her over.

"How may I help you?"

"I haven't seen or heard about Ren since you two had that argument. What's going on?"

Ty shook his head. "Ren's just a mess."

"But things are fine between the two of you?"

"Of course." Ty gave Evelyn an odd look. "It's perfectly healthy for Ren and I to clash. It's what makes us a good team."

"How?"

"We're a complete package. Nothing left out of this mess, that's for sure."

"I just wish I could help more."

"Help Ren? I've told you before, leave it to me. There's far too much of him to worry over."

"Then maybe it takes two or three."

"It does, but not all in the same way. I'm the one who deals with the chaos inside of Ren, the things he carries that no one else can understand. Jacquelyn may seem to stay in the background, but she keeps us both going with her quiet support and stability. Any time we need her, she's there."

"So what's my job?"

"You tell me." Ty pointed at her. "The truth is, you and I are a lot alike, which means you can be a great asset to Ren. Right now, learn how to keep everything going. We need extra people ready to come forward to do the tough jobs. Your knowledge of and experience with each of us doing our duties could prove to be useful should anything happen to us."

"I could never fill your shoes, so don't let anything too terrible happen to you."

"We try, but nothing can be certain. Awful things do happen. That's why I'm so worried about you."

"About me? Why?"

"I'm training you to take care of yourself because you're in as much constant danger as any of us. If you can defend yourself, it could save you from a lot, but that doesn't mean there won't be pain. It's hard. It's really, really hard." Ty's eyes held the look of someone who had felt pain before, and knew what it was to be haunted by it. "Are you prepared to handle it? Because we can't keep you from it. Fighting Scaolust means pain of any kind you can imagine. They're good at implementing the worst. What you fear most is sure to be what you'll get."

"You really expect I'll be going up against people who want to kill me?"

"Absolutely."

"Wow." The gravity of it hit Evelyn right then. "How are you going to get me ready for that?"

"I can't. I can train you physically, but I can't get inside your head. That's your job. Mental attitude is everything. I may be the best sword fighter in the castle, but if I panic, I'm finished. If I give up, I'm finished. I've learned to want to live more than Scaolust wants to kill me." He looked her in the eye. "You can develop that mindset, but it takes determination."

"Doesn't it go both ways though? What if my mindset is right but I don't have the skill set?"

"You'll get hurt. You'll probably get hurt anyway. Here in training, we try not to hurt each other. When we're out in real battle, it's exactly the opposite. You'll never experience it fully until it happens in the heat of the moment, and I can't prepare you to be beaten over the head, have your leg cut off, or be run through by an enemy blade."

Evelyn was getting chills just thinking about it. Ty sincerely believed it was possible that these things could happen to any one of them.

"It's up to you in those situations to keep your head. All I can do is warn you that it will be harder than anything else you've ever done or will do, train you the best I can, then send you to war." Ty led her out of the room and shut the door. "So do yourself a favor and meditate on it now. Picture what that pain will feel like and how you'll deal with it because you are going to need to deal with it someday."

29

If he could just get out of the castle before Ty caught him, Ren would be fine. He'd make himself be fine. He had duties to perform, promises to keep.

It's one thing to get past Ty in good health. It's another thing entirely to get past him with a bad leg slowing you down and making you clumsy. Luckily, Ren knew that Ty was keeping busy. If the prince wasn't with his brother, he was busy with the girls or his friends in the training area.

At first, Ren had tried to ignore the signs that he was getting weaker. When they refused to be ignored, he tried to hide it and convince himself that he could cope. This was growing progressively more difficult. Virgo's shot at Ren's leg had been far more intentional than Ren had realized for quite some time. Recently he'd realized the magic was still active, working at wearing away his health. Ren didn't like watching himself deteriorate.

Ren stopped to rest and leaned on a wall. His timing was bad. Ty and the girls came around the corner at the same moment. Ren stood up again, but not quickly enough to avoid raising Ty's suspicion. Ren wished he could avoid eye contact with his brother.

"Where are you off to?" Ty asked.

There was no point in lying. "The village," Ren responded. "I promised them I'd check in once a week until we have time to appoint a new governor." The last governor had been killed by Philomena. "Their normal issues are still important, regardless of our bigger problems."

"Well then, we've got nothing else to do. We'll come with you."

Ren was horrible at making excuses. Though he wanted to keep them all away and needed to rest, he only nodded and started walking again.

His effort to keep up with Ty's long, quick strides was valiant, really, but unsuccessful. The group continued to slow down for Ren until even Evelyn was making a conscious effort to stay beside Ren rather than go ahead of him. The girls watched his struggle with concern, but Ty, as any good brother would, glared at Ren until he finally caved and found a place to sit down, out of breath.

Ty stood with his arms crossed, staring at Ren, waiting for him to talk. Jacquelyn stayed quiet. Evelyn, on the other hand, wasn't waiting for an admission or explanation.

"That's gotten worse."

"What has?" Ren demanded defiantly.

"Your limp. Walking hasn't done this to you before."

"It's just all the stress." Ren looked at Ty. "I'm fine."

"Mhm." Ty jerked his chin up. "Let's see your leg."

"I said I'm fine."

"Don't care." Ty started towards Ren. The king moved to stop him but Ty shoved him back down. "Would you knock it off?" He pulled up Ren's pant leg and both girls gasped. Evelyn slapped a hand over her mouth and Jacquelyn closed her eyes.

Ren sighed and slumped back in the chair in defeat as Ty looked up at him. "What would you do without me?" It wasn't a joke. Ty hadn't expected it to be this bad.

"Just leave it alone."

"No." Ty was still studying the mass of black that covered Ren's leg. Evelyn had gotten the courage to venture forward and look too. Her face twisted.

"Ren, it looks like it's moving."

"I know it is, it's *my* leg."

Ty finally covered it again and stood up. "How long has it been getting worse?"

"I assume as long as it's been there."

"How long have you noticed?"

"Long enough to know that I am perfectly fine."

"Fine? Ren, it's practically eating you alive!"

"Well what do you want me to do about it? There's no way to fix this."

"We'll see about that." Ty pulled Ren to his feet. The expression on Ren's face as he struggled to stand shot straight to Evelyn's heart. She couldn't imagine trying to hide something like that.

"I know one thing," Ty continued. "You are not going to the village."

"I made a promise, Ty."

"We'll keep your promise for you." Ty turned to the girls. "Go check on the village for Ren, will you?"

Jacquelyn took Evelyn's arm and they hurried away. "They can handle it." Ty started helping Ren back to the library. "Why would you think it would be a good idea to keep this from me?"

"Because of what you just did. I have to be able to do my job."

"Looks like you're just going to have to learn to do your job differently."

"It includes far too many physical aspects."

"Like what? What do you need to do that I can't take over for you?"

"Fight. Do you expect me to just sit in my room alone during a war and hope for the best? Defenseless?"

"Yes, I do. And you won't be defenseless. I'll take care of that."

"You'll need to be out there leading for me." Ren groaned, half in pain, half in frustration. "I'm supposed to protect, not need protecting."

"I'm not staying with you, of course I'll be too busy for that. I'll just assign Evelyn to protect you. She seems to do a fine job of that."

"Very funny, Ty."

"Funny, yes, and yet strangely true."

"Only twice. And the first time doesn't count."

"Whatever you say."

"Ty."

"What?"

"We can't fix this. It's never going to stop getting worse."

Ty was silent.

30

Evelyn did as Ty told her to and was faithful to spend time training every day. Sometimes he was there with her, other times he couldn't be. Then Evelyn practiced alone.

It was on one of the days she was alone that Evelyn ran into Ren, again trying to get through the halls by himself, and having a horrid time of it. When he noticed Evelyn, he stopped and waited for her to catch him.

"Where is Ty?" she asked suspiciously.

"I was going to ask you the same thing. I was going to ask him for permission to visit the village today."

Evelyn smiled at the comment, satisfied that Ren wasn't going to hurt himself. "Jacquelyn and I have been keeping up on that for you, and by the looks of it, you're in no better condition than you were."

"No, I'm not going to be."

"I thought Ty was going to help with that."

"We tried. There's no way to cure this. But anyway, it's a better day than usual so I thought I would try to do something."

"You shouldn't push yourself like that. Don't you trust me on these things?" Evelyn teased.

"Of course I do, but I have a duty. Ty understands that."

"We all understand it. That's why we try to keep you from doing silly things like this."

"If you're this adamant, what are my chances with Ty?"

"Slim. But I'd be happy to help you find him."

"Of course you would."

Evelyn didn't want to let Ren keep wandering the castle alone, so she did go with him, stopping every now and then when he needed a break. The two came across plenty of various servants, but Ty was nowhere to be found. Evelyn noticed Ren's energy wearing thin.

"By the time we find him you're not even going to want to go anymore," Evelyn broke their silent search.

"I don't even know why I'm asking him." Ren collapsed to the floor to sit right where he was. He looked up at Evelyn. "I could order you to take me to the village right now and not tell anyone about it."

"Why the need to keep it a secret if you're so in charge?" Evelyn played back.

"Ty will let me do whatever I want, but I'll never hear the end of it if he doesn't approve."

Evelyn sat next to him. "I think if you and Ty didn't have so much pressure, you'd be a lot like me and my brother."

"You have a brother?"

"Yes, Nikolai. He's not quite as energetic or endearingly overbearing as Ty, but there was never anyone there for me as much as he was. I could very well have done without friends because I had my brother taking care of me."

"Ty's exactly the same for me. He has always filled every void in my life. I can't imagine losing him. I'm sorry we can't help you be with your brother."

Evelyn shrugged, sorry she had brought it up. "Luckily, I get to share yours."

"That is lucky."

"Why, are you bad at sharing?"

"Ty's too important to risk sharing. But you seem harmless enough," Ren joked.

"There you are." Ren and Evelyn looked up at the sound of Ty's voice. "I've been looking everywhere for you. What are you doing?" Ty stood over them.

"Evelyn and I haven't talked for a while," Ren responded. "Don't you think it's rude of me to ignore our guest?"

"It's rude for you to sneak off without telling me. And

Evelyn's not a guest anymore, she's one of us, so that excuse is invalid." Ty gave Ren a hand and pulled him to his feet. Then he turned to Evelyn. "What was he up to?"

"Actually, he was looking for you."

"Ah, good. I need him, too."

Ren looked suspicious. "What's wrong?"

Ty sighed. "I found something we forgot to take into account in our plans."

"How big of a problem is it?"

Ty shrugged. "Big enough that we need to start over."

Ren kept his mouth shut, trying to keep his frustration hidden. The silence was uncomfortable. Finally, Ren said, "Scaolust could attack us any time. We can't afford to make mistakes like this."

"We can't afford to fail because we were too hasty with our preparations."

"It's just a race to the attack."

"Is it? It doesn't look to me like they plan on having an all-out war."

Evelyn was confused. "Why isn't Scaolust attacking if it would be so easy for them to wipe us out?"

"They're having fun," Ty told her. "They don't have to worry, so they're torturing us in a sense."

"In a sense?" Ren's frustration was still building. "This *is* torture. They've killed innocent people, people who trust me to protect them, they've completely crippled me, and they've directly attacked us, the leaders. Yet we're all still alive. Isn't that the point of torture? To make death seem more merciful than life?"

"There's so much to live for, Ren," Ty said quietly. "Don't give up on me."

Ren stood there without a word for a moment, then turned and started for the library. Ty sighed and turned to Evelyn.

"How did Ren act towards you?"

"What do you mean?"

"Was he this tense?"

"I'm sure he was, but he didn't act like it."

"I wish I wasn't always bringing him bad news. Scaolust has always been a threat, but it's never been this bad. We used to be able to enjoy each other more. It hasn't always been this stressful."

"You aren't the one causing it." Evelyn put her hand on Ty's shoulder, bringing his eyes back to hers. "You're his brother. I'm a guest. He doesn't have to put on an act for you."

"I know. But you're not just a guest. I'm serious." Ty took her hands in his. "You're important. To all of us."

"Then why does he treat me differently?"

Ty smiled. "You're no sibling of Ren's, either, Evelyn." He squeezed her hands, then let them fall and started after his brother.

31

"Now begins the true test of what you've learned."

For several weeks Evelyn and Ty had been working intensely to get her skills up to par. Scaolust was surprisingly still leaving them alone long enough for their hard work to pay off. Evelyn was proud of herself and Ty was pleased and impressed. "Are you ready for this?"

"Absolutely." Evelyn was almost as excited as Ty. It was hard to believe a few weeks ago she had been so doubtful about training with him.

"Good." Ty grinned and pulled out his own weapon. Jacquelyn giggled on the sideline as Evelyn's jaw dropped.

"Wait! I have to face *you*?"

"Of course. What did you think the test would be?"

"I don't know, nothing this difficult."

"You'll be fine. I won't hurt you."

Evelyn didn't care. She was not ready for this, especially not with real weapons. "I can't do this yet, Ty."

"Sure you can."

"No, I really can't."

Ty shrugged. "Too bad you never have a choice in these matters." He lunged at her and Evelyn panicked. She darted out of the way. "Just keep your cool," he reminded as he came at her again. This time she blocked him, hands trembling a bit. "There you go."

Ty let Evelyn get over her nerves before he slowly began to build the intensity of their fight. Evelyn was soon breathless, but at this point there was no going back. She wasn't about to get beat because she quit, and Ty wouldn't let her get away. She had half an idea that he would still come after her if she called it quits and went upstairs.

And so the battle wore on, heightening more by the

minute. Ty was obviously enjoying the match. Evelyn was surprised she was able to hold out this long against him. Then again, he *had* trained her, and with a high goal in mind.

If any other person had done it, Ty would have called it sheer luck. But when Ty stood with his hands up in surrender, laughing at a shocked Evelyn pointing her dagger at him after knocking his weapon out of his hand, he was truly happy to be beaten.

Evelyn lowered her weapon slowly, suspicious of Ty. "There's no way I actually did that."

"No, you really did that. Enjoy this moment because it'll never happen again."

"I beat you?"

Ty nodded. "Well, sort of anyway."

"Sort of? What do you mean-" Evelyn was cut off as Ty jumped into action again, rendering her useless in a matter of seconds with his bare hands. "That's not fair!" Evelyn complained. "We never worked on that."

"I'm just making a point. In a real fight, don't ever hesitate. Anyone with any determination won't let you get away with hesitating." He paused. "But good job not killing me just now, that's not what practice is for."

She hugged him, still thrilled beyond belief, and he laughed at her enthusiasm.

"See, I told you it was amazing. Don't you love it?"

"I do love it." She pulled away. "It's like you've turned me into a child again."

"A lethal child." Raising his eyebrows, Ty beckoned her to follow him. "I have something for you."

Evelyn followed him to a small room off to the side. He made her wait outside the room and came back out with a small bundle wrapped in cloth. "You've earned this," he said, handing her the bundle. "I'm proud of all the work you've put into learning as much as you could in such a short amount of time."

Evelyn unfolded the cloth, revealing two beautiful daggers of her own. They glimmered as she pulled them out, intricate engravings flashing as she turned them. Ty also gave her a belt to wear in which she could carry them with her all the time. It was an incredibly thoughtful and perfect gift.

"Now I'll really be safe," she said. "These are amazing, Ty."

"I hope you don't have to use them often. But if you do, I know you'll wield them well."

32

Ty finally agreed to let Ren visit the village once—and only once—if he was careful and allowed Ty to help him no matter how embarrassing he thought it was. He also had to obey all of Ty's commands to stop and rest. For the most part, Ty didn't regret his decision. Things seemed to be going smoothly, and everyone was encouraged by the presence of their king.

Then bursts of black magic began to appear over the tops of trees in the forest. A growl of frustration escaped Ren. "Seriously?"

"I'll take care of it." Ty took off through the forest and Ren followed him slowly, not willing to be left behind.

Inside the forest, Evelyn ducked into a hiding spot and tried to quiet her breathing. She heard Philomena laugh, too close for comfort. Evelyn had been caught completely off guard, and Philomena had dragged her to the forest by the time she'd gotten her wits about her.

Evelyn located Philomena through the brush. She wanted to be on the offensive this time. Being caught by Philomena again would be regretful. Evelyn lashed out, and Philomena turned and blocked her. "You're going to have to do better than that."

Philomena shot her dark magic at Evelyn, who tried her best to dodge the blasts. Philomena was just taunting her. Even with Ty's training Evelyn couldn't combat magic effectively. It was only a matter of time before Philomena tired of mocking Evelyn and did away with her.

Philomena hit Evelyn, knocking her to the ground. Philomena pulled out her own dagger and advanced on her prey.

Evelyn crawled backwards on her hands, searching desperately for her own weapons, knocked loose in battle.

Philomena was close enough now. She kicked Evelyn down again and raised her weapon.

The sound of metal slicing the air caused Philomena to delay for the slightest moment. Ty's sword came down on her. Evelyn gasped and shuddered as he struck home.

Philomena fell to the ground as Ty pulled his sword free. He stood over Philomena for a moment, then turned to Evelyn, who was still in a state of shock. He knelt by her side. "Are you alright?"

Relief washed over Evelyn all at once. "I am now." She shook her head. "I'm still not strong enough."

"You're strong enough, you're just unsure of yourself. You need more confidence." Ty stood and pulled Evelyn to her feet, keeping a hand on her arm to stabilize her. "You're sure you're alright?"

Philomena was weak. Bleeding, dying, but not gone yet. She clawed at the ground, half blinded by pain, until her hand clutched her dagger again. Her magic was leaking away with her life, she could no longer use it. Each breath came harder than the last. She was determined to spend her last moments tearing Heretrua apart.

Philomena gathered her strength, grabbed Ty's ankle, and yanked him to the ground. The sheer surprise of the moment and Philomena's determination gave her enough momentum to plunge her dagger into him as Evelyn screamed.

Evelyn rushed to Ty and knelt over him. He gasped desperately, breathing raggedly. He clutched Evelyn's hand and squeezed it tight with all that was left in him as life slipped away from him.

Evelyn grasped his hand with both of hers as panic flooded her. "No, no, no, Ty, you'll be okay. Don't leave us."

A few small beams of sunlight filtered through the trees and sparkled on the young prince's face. He was dead, that was plain to see, however unwilling Evelyn was to believe it.

"Ty, we need you. You're going to be fine, we just..." Evelyn broke down sobbing, leaning on his body. He was still warm, still strong, still himself, but Ty was gone.

Ren's voice called out from beyond Evelyn's view. She looked up as he came into sight, slowly limping through the trees.

When he reached Evelyn and saw what she was bent over, he didn't say a word. His face lost all expression. He knelt next to Evelyn in a stupor, staring at the body of his brother. Ren touched Ty's lifeless hand and shook his head slowly.

"No." He held Ty's hand in his with a desperate grip. "No, this can't happen. Not you first, Ty."

Evelyn was silent, letting tears stream down her face as wave after wave of sorrow washed over Ren. He was paralyzed by loss.

Philomena's ragged breathing came back into focus. Ren lifted his head to see where she was laying, still somehow holding on to life.

"Victory," she gasped, looking at Ren triumphantly.

"Shut up!" Ren stood and kicked the dagger from Philomena's hand, feeling no pity when she moaned in pain. He felt himself choking on rage and sorrow.

Evelyn watched Ren kneel by Philomena as tears burned and clogged her throat. He picked Philomena's dagger up off the ground and held it in her face as she had done to him when she revealed herself. "You'll suffer for that," Ren hissed.

Evelyn hid her face in Ty's chest as Ren ended Philomena's life. How much pain Ren wanted to inflict on

Philomena frightened Evelyn. She didn't know how to help him. She didn't even know how to survive this herself.

Ren stood and faced away from the scene. He couldn't bear to look at Ty that way. He stood there in blind agony until he felt Evelyn's touch on his shoulder.

"Ren..."

He still didn't move.

In the same boldness and care that had been Ty's fashion, Evelyn wrapped her arms around Ren and leaned into his shoulder, allowing tears to course down her cheeks. Ren felt his anger sliding into grief against his will, yet somehow it was a relief to grieve.

At last Ren turned and held Evelyn in his arms, letting her be a comfort to him. Locked in the embrace, they mourned together in the stillness of the forest.

33

Ty's funeral was held on the brightest day of that week. Blue skies and singing birds seemed to mock the mourners. Ty would have loved that day, had he been alive to see it. As it was, everyone wished it would just start raining.

Of course, the turnout was huge. People poured in from all corners of the realm to pay their respects. They meant well, but no one at the castle wanted to take care of masses of mourners. It was all they could do to hold themselves together.

Ren especially struggled not to be rude, but found that sometimes he just couldn't make himself care for people and left it to the girls. He was still recovering from the blow that had finally proven to be too much. His brother had been his best friend. Ty was the only person Ren could bare his soul to. Now he felt lost and alone.

Scaolust loomed over them worse than ever. The shadow of the dark castle seemed to creep across the meadow further every day. Ren's hatred gave way to grief, but without Ty to press him onward, Ren seemed to have lost any will to fight. Had he given up? The girls left him to his seclusion for the time being, giving him time to recover in hopes that he would return to them able to pick up the fight again.

As king, Ren had no choice but to preside over the funeral. The last thing in the world Ren wanted to do was officially send away his brother forever. His duty was to acknowledge the death and yet make people believe things would somehow be okay again. But they could never be okay without Ty.

Ren ended up using his leg as an excuse to get away from everyone. Indeed, it was looking ever worse. Evelyn helped him sneak out, made sure he was alright, then snuck away herself.

Outside in the fading sunlight, Evelyn finally found peace. She pulled out one of the daggers Ty had given her and lovingly ran her fingers over the engravings. She wasn't ready to accept that he really wasn't coming back, though time and time again she had thought she was ready. She just didn't want it to be true. It was like he was away on a long trip, and if they just waited long enough, he would come back.

Genne had followed Evelyn outside and slipped her little hand inside Evelyn's. Suddenly Evelyn had the urge to share everything with the little girl. She hadn't spilled her emotions to anyone. She hugged Genne for a long time before the girl asked, "Will you teach me to fight like Ty, too?"

"That sounds like a great idea."

The girls sat in the tall meadow grass together and watched the stars come out one by one. They talked like equals, like friends, long into the night. Genne understood what it was like to lose someone like Ty. These two friends had both been torn from their lives without warning and were thrust into a new one. But at least now they were together.

After carrying Genne to bed, Evelyn tapped on Jacquelyn's door. When she received no answer, she tiptoed in. Jacquelyn was sitting on her bed, gazing into space. Evelyn crawled up next to her. "How are you doing?" she murmured.

"I'm scared of life without Ty," Jacquelyn whispered. "I'm scared we may get over this. I'm worried about Ren, what choices he'll make now, what he'll be like. I haven't just lost Ty. I've lost both of my brothers." She turned to face Evelyn. "It hurts."

Evelyn held Jacquelyn, tears they had held inside for days

flowed freely now. "I don't know what I'd do if you weren't here, Evelyn."

"Ren will recover. We just have to give him time." Ty's words echoed in Evelyn's mind. "He has carried so much weight he thinks no one else can understand or share with him. Ren keeps all the most difficult burdens locked away. Ty was the only one he shared with. We have to be patient. We have to show Ren that we can share and understand, too."

34

But Ren didn't recover. He secluded himself from the rest of the world, and no one heard from him. The castle seemed empty. Evelyn wandered around it alone. There was not much business to take care of, other than continuing to keep Ren's promise to the village. The people still had needs there.

Days passed in a blur. Evelyn still visited the training area daily, taking Genne often and picking out Ty's closest friends to work with them. They formed a recovery group that way, honoring what Ty had taught them to do.

Though their hearts remained sore, the other members of the castle slowly began to recover. But not Ren. He still didn't show himself or make any effort to return to normal life. Evelyn tried not to be frustrated with him, but her irritation was growing. They needed him to come back.

It seemed miraculous that Scaolust was still holding off. Evelyn knew Ren should be thinking about war, and that he wasn't currently doing so.

She did stumble across the plans he and Ty had been working on in the library. Evelyn was impressed by how much work was necessary to build a strategy. It must be intimidating to tackle alone.

It was hard to tackle life in general with the same energy as before. A hole had been cut out of each and every heart, a hole that could never be filled again.

Scaolust didn't wait for Ren's recovery to strike again. Evelyn, Jacquelyn, and Genne were in the village when a small group of men from Scaolust came out of the forest and attacked. As chaos broke out, Evelyn sent Genne away to the other side of the village and went forward to face the enemy with Jacquelyn.

Evelyn envied Jacquelyn's magic. No one could get close to her, while Evelyn had to get dangerously close to physically engage her opponents. Ty's training had paid off though. No one got past Evelyn.

However, Ty's predictions also came true. Evelyn got her first taste of pain—the searing burn of a deeply cut arm. Shock and the intensity of the moment distracted Evelyn from the pain as she carried on.

All at once, an explosion of blackness burst between the enemies, knocking everyone back. Virgo stepped out of the darkness. He stilled his men and approached Evelyn with his hands in the air. "I don't want to fight," he called. "I want to make a bargain."

Evelyn looked to Jacquelyn. Why wasn't he talking to the princess? "Fine, but you can talk from where you are. Stop moving."

Virgo obeyed and smiled. "I trust you will take this message directly to Rennigan without error or delay."

Evelyn nodded. "I will."

"Good. Here is the bargain. If the king will surrender himself, the princess, and you," he pointed at Evelyn, "into our hands, there will be no more war. No more death. We will stop this cat and mouse game we've been playing. Scaolust will take over peacefully and the people will live. Your lives for theirs. Otherwise, there will be no mercy for anyone."

"What kind of king do you think Ren is?"

Virgo shrugged. "Maybe he's not as unreasonable as you seem to think he is. This offer is the best you'll get. Rennigan will know that. He may consider it."

"What happens until we answer you?" Evelyn didn't trust Virgo.

"We'll stop this nonsense. Give him time to consider. I believe we've demonstrated all we need to." With another explosion of black magic, Virgo and all his men were gone except for the dead and injured ones. Useless to Virgo, they were left behind.

Evelyn looked down at the daggers in her hands. They were covered in blood. Her stomach turned as she looked at the men laying on the ground. She had done this to them.

All at once, Evelyn's arm burned fiercely. She put her other hand over the cut and squeezed tight to try to relieve the pain. Jacquelyn was soon at her side. "What happened?"

"I got cut. I'm scared to look at it."

"That bad?" Jacquelyn held out her hand. "Let me see."

Evelyn held out her arm, the hand she unwillingly pulled off of it wet, dripping with blood. Evelyn closed her eyes and shuddered, trying not to think about it as Jacquelyn examined it.

"Evelyn, that's really bad."

"What is?" Genne appeared out of nowhere and looked at Evelyn's arm. "Ew."

"Can you go get me some water and a rag?"

"And the doctor," Evelyn added, nodding to the men on the ground. "Some of them aren't dead."

Evelyn finally got up the courage to look at her arm by the time Genne was back. There was far more blood than she had realized, preventing them from properly analyzing the injury. Jacquelyn had to assure Genne it was fine, comforting Evelyn at the same time.

Jacquelyn rinsed the wound repeatedly, examining it between rinsing. "It's really deep."

Jacquelyn rinsed it one more time, pressed the rag over it before more blood could flow, and tied it tightly. Evelyn felt warmth spreading from the princess' hand to her wound, and the pain began to numb.

"What are you doing?" she asked Jacquelyn.

"I can't heal things, but I can numb pain with my magic," the princess explained.

"What if it gets infected?"

Jacquelyn shook her head. "I can't take care of that, either. Try not to worry about it."

"I can help with that." The doctor approached Evelyn. "Looks like that's all I'll need to do, you're already in good hands." He pulled out some dried leaves and handed them to Jacquelyn. "I won't make you take the bandage off already, but put these on it when you do change it." He turned to Evelyn again. "Now what else can I do for you?"

"I need you to inspect those men," Evelyn said, pointing. "Some of them are still alive. They need your help."

"But they're..." the doctor began to protest, but Evelyn interrupted him.

"I know. It doesn't matter. We'll find something to do with them."

"You know some of them will be beyond helping."

Evelyn looked at them again. "Sort them out. I'll take care of the ones you can't."

The doctor nodded and got to work.

Evelyn looked at her bandaged arm. "This is only the beginning, isn't it?"

Jacquelyn nodded and Evelyn fought back the defeat threatening to wash over her.

The patients the doctor selected were taken away to a more comfortable setting. When the area cleared, Evelyn knelt next to one of the men left. Jacquelyn sat beside her. "What are you going to do?"

Evelyn studied the face of the man before her. His expression pierced her heart. It didn't matter where he was from, he was another human being, completely at her mercy. In all the time Evelyn had been here, she never imagined this would be her job. It shouldn't be her job.

"Why didn't the doctor take me?" he whispered weakly.

Evelyn looked him in the eye. He was so afraid, and in so much agony. "He can't help you," she replied softly. "I'm sorry."

"What are you going to do now?"

Evelyn turned to Jacquelyn. "Can you help make it less painful?"

In response, Jacquelyn brought a soft glow to her hands and numbed the spot of the injury as much as she could.

The man was obviously afraid, he was shaking and his eyes were shut tight. "It's going to be okay," Evelyn reassured him, taking his hand in hers."Just breathe."

He obeyed. Evelyn waited, listening to his breathing as it became gradually slower, and shallow, each breath farther from the last.

"Jacquelyn, can you do the same for all the others?" Evelyn whispered softly. The princess got off her knees and did as requested.

Finally the man's breathing stopped entirely.

Ren is out of time to get over it, Evelyn thought.

35

By the time Evelyn returned to the castle, she was furious. She did not care if Ren wanted company or not. All the servants knew they would be wise to tell her where he was without protesting. Evelyn stormed into Ren's hidden refuge and slammed the door.

"I just killed fifteen people," she declared. "How are you?"

Hands on hips, she stood in front of him expectantly, containing her fury for a moment, though it was painted all over her face. Ren looked at her in disbelief.

"What happened?"

"It doesn't matter," Evelyn fumed. "You know what does?"

Ren shook his head, still baffled by her sudden entrance and shocking announcement.

Evelyn slammed her hand down on the table. Ren jumped. "You didn't even realize your own village was being attacked! You don't even care!"

"That's not true."

"Stop lying to me. When Ty was alive you were adamant about visiting the village, keeping your promises. Now you're never there for them. For anyone!" Evelyn collected herself and crossed her arms. "Virgo sent a message for you."

"What happened to your arm?"

Evelyn looked down at the blood-soaked rag wrapped around her arm. "Did you hear what I said? Virgo sent you a message."

"Through you?"

"Yes, through me. He wants to bargain with you."

"What did he say?"

"If you surrender yourself, Jacquelyn, and me into his hands, Scaolust will take over Heretrua peacefully and no one will die. Otherwise, there's going to be war, and he'll show no mercy."

"So our three lives for the lives of all our people?" Ren looked as if he were considering this offer.

"What's that look for?"

"It is something we should consider."

"Have you lost your mind?"

"No!"

"Really? Because it's starting to look like it."

Ren was indignant. "You have no right to-"

"Don't start with that, Ren. Since Ty died, you've lost all sense of responsibility, any shred of hope, and your lack of leadership makes me wonder if you were ever the one running the show."

Ren stood up and opened his mouth, but got no words out.

"I'm not done!" She started pacing furiously. "I saw your plans in the library. Ty talked to me about you all the time. I know how often you two were together, how much you discussed and bantered back and forth. I know how much he loved you, and what that meant to you. But you can't let your hope die with your brother." Evelyn stopped in front of Ren, looking him square in the eye. "I don't know what you plan on doing now, but I know what Ty would think of you if he were here. And I know which of us he would agree with, too." With those words, Evelyn stomped out the door.

36

Evelyn felt a little guilty as she walked to the village the next day. Had she overstepped her bounds with Ren? He had deserved it, and she had only told him the truth. Someone had to tell him the truth.

The events of the past day still left Evelyn numb and angry. She shouldn't have been put in that awful situation.

Ren was probably upset with her, too. But if he couldn't deal with Scaolust, surely he wasn't going to bother confronting Evelyn.

Genne ran up to Evelyn as soon as she spotted her, excitement spilling over as she called, "Evelyn, guess what?" She came to a halt in front of Evelyn. "Look!"

Evelyn followed Genne's pointing finger, her eyes resting on Ren. "How long has he been here?"

Genne was obviously thrilled. "I don't know. But everyone is so happy to see him!"

A crowd had gathered around Ren. Genne helped Evelyn push through them to his side. He stood up when he saw Evelyn. She came close enough to speak to him without anyone else hearing. "What are you doing here?" she questioned. "You're in no condition to be-"

Ren held up his hands. "I know, I know. But where else did you want me to start?"

"What do you mean?"

"Look, I understand I've been irresponsible. This may not be what you had in mind, but it's the only place I knew I could start."

"You aren't going to be much use if you push yourself too far."

"I can't do everything yet. I can't plan a war, I don't even want to." He had lowered his voice to the slightest of murmurs. "I don't see any point in fighting anymore. Even if I did, my help is gone."

Evelyn looked at his worn out, heavy burdened eyes and softened. "You need to stop keeping everything to yourself. Life is meant to be shared, burdens and happiness alike."

Evelyn slid her hand in Ren's elbow to give him support. "Jacquelyn and I are here to help you get through anything."

She turned to the crowd around them. "I need to speak to the king alone," she told them.

The crowd parted as Evelyn led Ren away from the village into the meadow for peace. She was going to make sure he kept fighting, but Evelyn wasn't going to let him fight alone any longer.

37

Evelyn quickly became Ren's shadow. She stepped up to fill the holes Ty's absence left in every way she possibly could. She was Ren's emotional support and stability, his advisor, his motivation (which often meant she had to go on tangents and rants like Ty had), and even his physical help. Though Ty was still missed, Ren began to appreciate and connect to those close to him who were still living. Normality returned aside from the occasions someone would include Ty in a conversation only to remember he wasn't there.

The role Evelyn played in helping Ren he didn't want people to know about was her role as a literal crutch for him. As his condition continued to worsen, all the time he spent getting from place to place was wearing him down. Evelyn's concern led her to confront him about doing something about it.

"Well I'm not walking on a crutch," he insisted. "Firstly because I'm not ready to be brought that low already and secondly because no one can know how bad this is."

"Why not?"

"I'm their king. I can't be seen as weak. It's disheartening."

"Then you're going to need someone with you all the time so if it becomes too much they can help you."

"I'm not going to get hurt."

Evelyn crossed her arms.

"Look, I don't want company all the time. Sometimes it's nice to have privacy. I certainly don't want a babysitter."

"Fine. Then what about me?"

"What about you?"

"Would my company bother you? I can help as well as

anyone else and I'm probably more concerned. Besides that, I've got nothing else to do."

"That's not true, you've been half running this place on your own."

"I don't do quite that much, but you do have a point." Evelyn thought about it a moment. "I *don't* have anything *better* to do, anyway. Will I be a bother or not?"

"No, you won't bother me."

"You're sure? That's an awful lot of time with one person."

He smiled. "I'm sure I won't get tired of you, but you may get tired of me."

"Never."

Their new plan made almost everything inconspicuous. Ren's limp appeared to all outside views no worse than it had before. What *was* drawing attention was the fact that Ren and Evelyn were never seen apart from each other, and Evelyn's hand was always in Ren's elbow. People did begin to take note, and the two let them. It was better for people to gossip than to know that Ren could barely walk long distances alone.

A few weeks passed without Virgo returning. Everyone who knew about his offer knew their time had to be running out. Ren still tried desperately to find a solution. The stress he was under continued to grow, but Evelyn continued to believe in him and to prod him on. She was proud of how hard he had worked so far.

"I feel like I've exhausted every option," Ren complained to Evelyn in the library one day.

"You haven't, you've just emptied what's in your own brain. We'll just have to search harder for more."

"I can't."

"Nope, we're not doing that again." Evelyn crossed the room to where he was sitting. "Close your eyes and breathe."

Ren did as he was told and Evelyn continued talking. "We're sitting in a giant library. There's got to be something around here to help you. You've lived here your entire life, so I suspect you know where to send me to look if you'll just think about it for a minute."

Ren opened his eyes and pointed. "That shelf."

Evelyn got out a stool and started looking, calling out what she found so he could approve or disapprove. This had been their habit lately. Ren sat and worked while Evelyn ran around getting him what he needed and carrying orders to appropriate places. Not only were they planning for a war, they had to keep the kingdom running at the same time.

Finally Ren had what he needed and Evelyn sat down next to him. She set a rolled up scroll of paper on the table.

"I didn't ask for this," he said. "What is it?"

"The plans you were working on with Ty." Evelyn rolled them out. "Maybe they will help."

"Ah." He looked at it for a moment without moving, then pulled it to him. "Good idea." Ren went back to work.

"Are you ever going to answer Virgo?"

"I don't know."

"You're just trying to drag this out as long as you can, aren't you?"

"Yes and no. I am truly trying to find a solution, but we simply don't have the resources."

"Hm."

"I'm just tired, Evelyn."

She sat there silently for a moment before leaning her head on his shoulder. "Me too."

He put his arm around her. "We'll be okay."

Evelyn sighed. That all depended on his definition of

'okay.'

"I am getting impatient, I'll freely admit that." Ren and Evelyn both looked up at the sound of the new voice in the room. "You've had enough time to consider my bargain," Virgo said, "I've been quite generous with the amount of time I've given you. I'm here for your answer and I do expect one."

Ren stood, and Evelyn smiled inside at what she knew was Ren's silent way of showing Virgo his injury couldn't keep him down. It was rebellion. She also loved that Ren practically towered over the other king. However, she remained where she was, silent, waiting for Ren's response.

"When I received your offer, I did think it reasonable and fair. Beyond that, I believed it was the best and possibly only resolution we could come to, and would have agreed to it almost immediately."

"Would have?"

"My opinion has been swayed. Whether I've come to my senses or lost them, I'm not sure, but I can assure you that the decision is final."

"I thought you were a more sacrificial leader than that."

The words hit Ren, Evelyn could see that, but he was resolute. "I will not turn my people over to you, no matter how it is disguised."

"You'll turn them over to me by your inability to defeat me then."

"You're overconfident."

"I'm overconfident?" Virgo chuckled. "Haven't I proven to you who should be worried about confidence?" He moved around Ren threateningly. "I thought killing your brother would have made that point."

Now he really had Ren's attention.

"It's no use for you to fight. You may want to honor your

brother, you may not want to surrender, to admit defeat. But really, you're just falling for the same trap your brother did."

"Ty's fault wasn't his confidence. It was his willingness to sacrifice himself. His over-eagerness to help someone else."

"You have the same fault. I gave you a way out and you denied it, even though you had new freedom to choose what you knew was the best decision."

"Do you recall who else died that day? Ty killed Philomena, as well. Maybe I'll die in the act of killing you, just like my brother did, but you're still coming down with me. I deny your bargain, and will now serve you and all of your kingdom justice. That is what I desire."

"If that is what you want, why not give it to me now?"

Virgo pulled out a sword. Ren stepped back. "We can settle this right here. No more bargaining."

It was an unfair match. Ren wasn't in any condition to fight, so Evelyn jumped to her feet and attacked Virgo herself.

She proved to be a decent distraction. Virgo had to leave Ren alone in order to defend himself, and Evelyn knew enough to avoid his blows while still posing a threat to him. Ren took the opportunity to shoot the sword out of Virgo's hand and jump on his back. The two men stumbled to the ground, Ren trying to hold Virgo down. Evelyn didn't know what to do at this point.

Then Virgo stopped fighting Ren and started shooting his dark magic at Evelyn. She was defenseless against such power. It distracted Ren as Virgo had wanted it to, but Ren didn't weaken in the least. Instead, he shot his magic into Virgo as well, causing him to lose concentration as he yelled in pain and managed to kick Ren, hard.

Virgo was on his feet the minute Ren's hold broke. Virgo turned on Ren to kill him and Evelyn, still behind Virgo, threw her dagger across the room. She winced as it sunk into Virgo's shoulder.

That did the trick. The king of darkness vanished in a burst of black magic, getting away as fast as he could. Evelyn was happy to find that his magic wouldn't take the dagger in his shoulder with him. She hadn't wanted to lose Ty's gift.

Evelyn helped Ren to his feet. "How did you not die?" he asked her, out of breath.

"Same way I defended the village that one time when you were too busy sulking to know about it."

"Which I had not taken enough notice of. Evelyn." He put his hands on both of her shoulders. "What if I had lost you, too?"

"You didn't though, that's what matters. I can take care of myself pretty well, huh?"

"How? And where did you get those?" He pointed to her daggers.

"Ty." Evelyn answered both questions at once. "He gave them to me after I somehow managed to beat him in a duel. He trained me for quite some time."

"You beat Ty?"

Evelyn nodded.

"And you two kept all of this from me?"

She shrugged. "I guess there didn't seem to be any reason to tell you about it."

"I understand, beating Ty at his absolute favorite pastime isn't a big deal."

"You were busy with more important things."

"More important things?" Ren sighed and unexpectedly wrapped his arms around Evelyn. "They don't seem more important anymore."

38

Evelyn had sealed Heretrua's fate when she threw that dagger into Virgo's shoulder. It wasn't safe for Scaolust to taunt them anymore. Philomena had already been killed and Virgo barely escaped. Their next action was easy to predict.

"Can you teach me how to throw daggers next?" Genne had joined Evelyn and Jacquelyn in the princess' room to discuss the situation and was bouncing up and down on the bed after listening to Evelyn tell her latest story.

"What do you think Virgo will do now?" Jacquelyn looked concerned. Evelyn felt exactly the way she looked.

"Ren refused to surrender and I tried to kill him, so I presume he won't be messing around anymore."

"That's what I'm afraid of," Jacquelyn sighed.

Just then, Ren entered the room. "Scaolust has commanded our surrender," he announced, collapsing into a chair. "You know what refusal means."

The girls nodded.

"We can't withstand an attack from Scaolust." Ren leaned forward and put his head in his hands. "And I have nothing in the way of plans."

"That's not true," Evelyn protested. "We've been working hard on that."

"We still don't have anything that will work. We never would have, and we never will."

"Ren," Evelyn knelt on the floor next to him. "You have to stop losing hope and giving up when the action starts. We need you most when it gets intense."

"It's when the action starts that I realize how foolish it is to think we can win."

"You have to let your crazy side come out. Pick the best option and go for it with all your heart."

"What else can I do?"

"Nothing. That's why you have to get crazy."

"I have to make a decision fast, but all of the options available have the potential to destroy us all. Not only us, but the entire realm."

"No pressure," Genne commented, still bouncing on the bed. Jacquelyn hushed her.

Evelyn reached out and took Ren's hand in reassurance. "No matter what you do, we'll all stick with you to the end."

"I know you will. You give me so much, why can't I give anything back to you? I can only offer you potential death in exchange for your support."

"Or an unexpected victory. Ren, stop feeling guilty and just use our support, because it's not going anywhere. This is not about any of us, it's about protecting the people who rely on you. Would you rather us die painfully fighting for their lives, or watch passively as we are all helplessly destroyed because we did nothing?"

He squeezed her hand. "It's still okay to be afraid."

Evelyn smiled. "Of course. We're all scared. If we make it out it won't be without scars. But if we fight through every last wound, we just might make it out alive. We've done it before. We can't let them get to our heads. That's what they're best at, it's their greatest and favorite weapon. We can beat that."

"You sound just like Ty."

Evelyn smiled wistfully. "If there was one thing he wanted to teach me to deal with, it was fear and pain. It's paralyzing, he knew that as well as anyone." Evelyn put both her hands around Ren's and looked up at him earnestly. "But you *can* be strong even when you're scared. Don't let your fears decide your fate. If you give up, we're all finished."

"Scaolust still has more power than us, it's just a simple

fact."

"They also have a strong desire to wipe us out. The best thing Ty ever told me was that we have to want to live more than Scaolust wants to kill us."

"Seems like it's hard to want anything more than Scaolust wants us dead."

"Believe in the impossible, Ren. Look at me. Everything about me is impossible. That I'm here in your world, that I picked the flower on your side, that Scaolust didn't kill me. You're just as impossible. Believe in the crazy for me, Ren."

39

Ren knew Heretrua was going down no matter what anyone did. There was only one person he wanted to talk to and though he was with Evelyn all the time, interruptions were constant. So he took her to one of the few places in the castle he hadn't shown her yet, the one place he knew they would be left alone as long as they needed. She protested that the towers were far too much of a stretch for him, but he insisted.

The climb was worth it when they finally reached the top. It was so quiet, undisturbed. Looking over the edge, they could see the meadow, the forest, the whole land that was Heretrua. It was beautiful.

Evelyn wished they could just enjoy this together, without having to worry about the other castle in sight, or the massive army waiting inside it.

"It's so frustrating." Ren ran his hands through his hair, leaving it rumpled. "I'm just sitting here waiting to watch everything I've fought for be destroyed. We're just waiting to die. And I can't do anything about it."

"You aren't giving up?"

"Of course not. I can't. But Evelyn." She looked up at him, the sound of his voice worrying her. "I have to be honest with you now. You know we can't send you home."

Evelyn nodded.

"Scaolust is going to destroy all of us. We'll fight to the very end, but there is truly nothing we can do to win. Heretrua isn't the only kingdom that will be wiped out, they'll destroy the entire realm, but they have to get through us first."

"You're sure you've exhausted every option?"

"I'm positive. I want to be hopeful, and I'm grateful

you've kept everyone else that way. I want to believe we can do this, but look at how short time is. What is stacked against us. I'm not going to lie to you when it's just the two of us. I can only tell you the truth and give you your options."

"I thought we didn't have any options."

"Yours are a little different than mine."

"How can they be different than yours?"

"Because I want to protect you from the worst of this." His eyes were earnest. "You can stay here with us if you choose, which means fighting alongside us. It's going to get ugly fast, and painful. I don't want you to have to experience that if I can give you a way out."

"I can handle anything you and Jacquelyn can. I would feel guilty leaving you to do this while I... well, what is my other option?"

I can send you to one of the smaller kingdoms. If you live with a poor family, you may be hidden and safe a little bit longer. You may even survive this. But Scaolust is after you, too, so you'd never be safe to reveal yourself again. You would always be running."

"So really, either way, we all die."

Ren just looked at her, not a shred of hope in his face. Evelyn wasn't going to leave them now. She wasn't going to give up hoping with and believing in them after she had challenged Ren to be hopeful and keep trying for so long.

"I'm staying here."

"You're sure about that?"

Evelyn nodded. "I don't see any reason to do otherwise."

"Don't count on what you wish to be true," Ren warned her. "If there was any chance we could make it through, I would tell you, I promise." He finally broke away from her eyes and looked over her head at the view. "I'm terrified,

Evelyn."

They were quiet for a moment. Only the distant sound of birds in the trees below could be heard.

"I'm glad you're staying." Ren finally broke the silence. "I need you by my side. Even if I die fighting it means something. I'll have done my job."

"You want to finish well."

"If we have to lose, I want to make them suffer while they're beating us." Ren met Evelyn's eyes again. "Now that I've told you the truth, now that you've made up your mind, knowing the odds-" he shook his head, focusing on what he had been going to say. "I need someone to push me through to the end. Someone to give me and the people the kind of strength and courage that comes straight from the heart." Ren slid his hand into Evelyn's, pulling her to him with his eyes. "Someone to give me what Ty had. Hope. The will to fight, even if there seems to be no point. You've given me all of that. You've been for me what Ty was. I can never repay you for that."

"You don't have to."

"But I've done nothing for you. Not only that, I want to ask you to do even more."

"What do you need from me?"

"I need someone to reach inside of me and pull out what I can't pull out of myself. Someone so close that they're practically a part of me. I wasn't looking for that before because I didn't realize that was what I really needed. I didn't know it was possible. I just wanted normal. I don't want normal anymore, Evelyn. I want you."

He smiled as he ran his hand over her hair. All at once Evelyn realized his gestures had been slowly outgrowing friendship to become this.

"You, with all your surprises and boldness, your ability to

tackle challenges, shocking me with something new every day, bending the rules, arguing with me when you should be keeping quiet." His hand came to rest at the back of her neck and a thrill went through Evelyn's body at his touch. "That's what I want. A hectic, chaotic, dangerous—a *real* love." He slowly slid his hand around Evelyn's waist and pulled her closer. His voice was soft and raspy. "And I want it with you."

Evelyn's heart was pounding hard. She was breathless in the moment, lost in Ren's eyes. He had a firm grasp on her very heart.

She pulled her thoughts into focus, trying to concentrate in the midst of overwhelming emotion. Ren was warm and strong and his arms were secure despite his failing health. Evelyn felt there what anyone would want to feel before they died—loved, needed, and protected to the end.

Ren tilted Evelyn's chin up. She was hit by the blueness of his eyes, the intensity and passion she found there. Ren had found something to live for and to fight for again.

He needed her, but more than that, he wanted permission to just love her, with all that was left in him. It was the best they could do with what was sure to be their last days living.

"You want me..."

Ren nodded and Evelyn laughed in disbelief.

"...to be *Queen* of Heretrua?"

He nodded again, laughing with her as he wrapped both arms around her, pulling her body close to his. Evelyn's breath caught in her throat as she looked up at him.

"I'd love that," she whispered.

A smile Evelyn had only seen on him once before lifted the strain right off the king's face. It was like the sunset, gentle, soft, majestic, like a sort of symphony. This smile, his true smile, was what Evelyn remembered from the first time she met him, that day he had been so pleased to finally see her and she had been awestruck by him.

Both timid, both eager—slowly, gently—their lips met. Goosebumps shivered over Evelyn's entire body as he held her there. Her heart raced with pure joy.

Light shot out from the couple in a circle. It sliced through Heretrua and the kingdoms beyond, rattling the foundations of the Scaolust castle. When the light hit the edges of Heretrua's realm, it bounced back and rushed into itself at the tower, then exploded into the sky. A wash of azure, amethyst, and amber filled the sky, even over Scaolust. Ren and Evelyn pulled apart and looked up at the colors.

"Did we do that?" Ren asked.

"I think so." Evelyn leaned into Ren. "It's the most beautiful thing I've ever seen."

"Second most beautiful thing I've ever seen," Ren responded, looking at Evelyn, then kissing the top of her head.

Neither one felt like leaving the tower, so they sat in the warmth of the sunlight and the peaceful silence provided by the tower's height. In those moments, those blissful, wonderful moments, they were just two ordinary people, finally able to love each other without a care in the world.

40

Evelyn felt a thrill of happiness go through her when she woke the morning after her wedding, still held in the king's embrace. It was a warm, perfectly comfortable moment that left her completely unwilling to move, lest she break the perfection.

The journey from Ren's proposal to this point had been exhilarating. The effort to keep the news quiet had been massive and preparations moved quickly. Ren and Evelyn wanted to enjoy life together as long as they could.

Evelyn had become fully aware of what she was doing, what she was becoming. With all their secrecy, few people outside of Heretrua even knew the wedding had taken place. If they did make it through the war, then what? Evelyn would still be their queen. She would have to prove herself to everyone. She was second only to Ren in the entire realm.

What if she made it through the war, but Ren didn't?

Now she understood the pressure and stress Ren felt all the time.

The ceremony and party after had been spectacular, better than any wedding Evelyn could have ever dreamed of on her own. Partly because of what it symbolized for the people—her people. The hearts of all who attended their wedding were joyful and celebratory.

The king and his new queen were well aware that the party lasted long into the night, but they left the noise early. They were grateful to have shared their joy with their people. Now they just wanted to love and enjoy each other in peace, each being for the other the only place they could truly find rest.

Now, in the stillness of the morning, Evelyn's fingers were starting to tingle. She moved slowly, trying not to wake

Ren. She rubbed her hands together to wake them up, then stopped and stared.

There was an amber glow in her palm. A surge of excitement went through Evelyn as she realized what it was.

Evelyn focused on bringing the magic now inside of her out. Soon she was forming beautiful spirals and swirls of light in the air. She could barely contain her excitement.

She focused on a lantern on the dresser, and it lit. Evelyn searched the room for all kinds of silly things to do to test out her magic. She was giddy. What had seemed like a fairy tale a few months ago was now her reality.

Ren started to stir and Evelyn quieted down, not wanting to wake him any earlier than he would on his own. She rolled back over to face him. As Ren settled in again, he managed to kick his own leg, and a brief flash of pain crossed his face.

It pricked Evelyn's heart and she examined it for herself. The black mass was huge and ugly. It continued to grow worse. She wished there was some way she could help him. Could she do something, anything, to give him any relief?

She put her hand on his leg and focused on using her magic to try to ease the pain. Maybe it couldn't be healed, but if she could numb it as Jacquelyn had done for Scaolust's men, it would be enough to satisfy Evelyn.

It was hard, exhausting. Evelyn had no idea what she was doing. The mass didn't actually change, but it did look less consuming to Evelyn. She sighed. That would have to do. She hoped Ren felt a difference and that she wasn't just imagining things.

She settled back in and closed her eyes to wait for Ren to wake up. It didn't take him long. Evelyn knew he was awake when he kissed the back of her neck and chuckled low in his throat at her surprise.

"Good morning, my love," he murmured in her ear.

She smiled and rolled over to face him again. "It's more like good afternoon now."

"I know. It was quite a party."

"I doubt it's safe to venture out yet," Evelyn joked. Ren smiled.

"Well, we could always just stay in here all day."

"That sounds wonderful," Evelyn agreed. "As long as we get breakfast fast."

Ren laughed. "You've been awake for awhile, haven't you? He sat up and swung his legs off the bed. "I'll take care of that now." He stood and stopped without taking a step. He looked down at his leg. "Have you seen this?"

Evelyn nodded, pleased that she had been of some use, then looked down as Ren examined it and gasped. The black mass was shrinking before their eyes until it was completely gone. No, she hadn't seen this.

Ren straightened. "What happened?" he demanded, astonishment burning inside of him.

Evelyn brought the glow to her hands again and showed him, still staring at his leg. "I have magic now."

Ren's face drained of all other expression other than utter shock. "You did this?"

"Yes." She looked up at him. "Why? Ren, what's wrong?"

Ren came back to Evelyn and took her hands, looking in her eyes searchingly, in disbelief. She was every bit as confused as he was.

"Only the Queen of Light can influence darkness," Ren said quietly.

41

Breakfast was forgotten. The royal couple spent the rest of their day studying Evelyn's magic, testing it and experimenting with it, almost afraid to believe she really possessed the power she seemed to, lest they be bitterly disappointed. They were like excited children at play. Evelyn had never seen Ren so overjoyed.

"And to think, I didn't even believe the Queen of Light would ever come. Now I'm married to her!"

Ren swept Evelyn off her feet. She laughed in pleased surprise as he spun her around. "This means we have a chance at defeating Scaolust again. And we will! We just have to use our time wisely."

"We don't have much time left."

"It's fine! We'll figure something out." He kissed Evelyn in the exhilaration of new hope. She was sure now, as he was, that they could find a way to put her power to use, fresh as it was and despite Evelyn's lack of experience.

Then Ren grew solemn. "What I would give to have Ty here to see this."

"He'd have an awful lot to gloat about."

"I wouldn't mind."

42

 They did not communicate with Scaolust in any way. They did nothing but study and work with Evelyn's magic. Most people with magic grew up learning how to use it, but Evelyn had to experiment and learn now. They had very little time. Handling so much power was difficult.

 The difficulty was not how to use enough power, but how to restrain it. Sometimes her magic spontaneously spilled out by itself. When Evelyn tried to use small amounts it would overwhelm her with too much. She had to control herself and her emotions to control her magic. She could not get frustrated, be careless, or speak too passionately, or out it came. So she, Ren, and Jacquelyn spent all their time on Evelyn's training.

 She soon learned to control her magic, rather than letting it control her. In spite of her clumsiness, the power within her was impressive. When she was in complete control of it, even more so.

43

Evelyn had not expected to ever willingly return to the Scaolust castle, but that was exactly what she had to do. This time it was a break-in.

One thing she had been particularly excited to learn was teleportation. It was comforting to know she could remove herself from any sticky situation she needed to.

Virgo was surprised when Evelyn showed up in his castle out of nowhere. However, he disguised his shock, as usual, with his smooth tone of voice. "Ah, a new one?" He stood. "Did they need you to replace Ty?"

"No one can replace Ty."

Virgo cocked an eyebrow, putting the pieces together. "Have you become Ren's queen then? How exciting."

Evelyn stood silent. Resolute.

"You're here to surrender?"

"You'll have to wait a long time for Heretrua to surrender to you."

"You're out of time."

"We understand that."

"You'll regret your decision."

"I won't be here to regret anything."

Virgo was confused again. "How so?"

"I'm surrendering myself to you," Evelyn said. "For Genne."

"Genne?"

"She's my maid. Only nine years old." Evelyn looked Virgo directly in the eye. "Philomena killed her mother and almost killed her."

"Do you think I have time to discover the identity of one child in order to spare her life so she can grow up to hate us, leaving the possibility of starting a rebellion in the future?"

"You're obviously very unstable if a nine year old can concern you," Evelyn commented. "Besides, you were prepared to let all of our people live if we surrendered to you."

Virgo grinned. "You believed that?"

"It's not as difficult as you make it seem. However, if you're that worried, turn her to the darkness the way Maserta did to you, but spare her life."

Virgo cleared his throat, looking uncomfortable at Evelyn's last statement. "Fine. Your life for hers." He smiled. "Good to have you back." He turned aside to speak to a man Evelyn hadn't even noticed was there. As Virgo talked, Evelyn closed her eyes and gathered focus and power.

As the man left on Virgo's errand, Evelyn brought swirling pools of power to the air above her hands.

Virgo turned back to her. "What are you doing?"

Evelyn let it all loose, directing the full force of her magic into Virgo. Shocked, then angered, he fought back, but couldn't touch Evelyn. They emptied the power in their hands, and both pulled out their material weapons at the same time.

Fighting Virgo was nothing like fighting his soldiers. The master had tricks up his sleeves Evelyn hadn't been warned about. It was hard to keep her head, but in the end, Evelyn came out on top.

Evelyn had never felt as sickened as she did when she plunged her dagger into Virgo's body without hesitation, as Ty had instructed.

Even this king of darkness was human. The expression on his face burned Evelyn's heart as she shot one more blast of light into him, knocking him away from her.

Knowing he had been rendered completely harmless, Evelyn knelt next to the dying king and used her magic to ease his pain.

"Why are you doing that?" he gasped.

Evelyn looked down at him. "I just killed you."

"Yes." He leaned his head back down to the floor with a moan. "But how?"

He was dying. It wouldn't hurt to tell him the truth. "I'm the Queen of Light."

"You are?" He smiled weakly, with seeming relief. "You'll win. At last."

Evelyn's eyes searched his for answers.

"When we met I lied to you. You don't ever get used to it, Evelyn. Just numb to it."

Virgo was changing back. In his last few minutes of life, Evelyn's light seeped into Virgo, healing his soul. "I'm sorry," Evelyn whispered.

He looked her straight in the eye. "Don't be. Good luck."

Ren was not happy with Evelyn taking on such a task without talking to him first, but the results wiped all of that away. He pulled her into his arms and hugged her tight for a long time.

"I think the command to surrender has just been reversed."

44

Evelyn couldn't sleep. Something wasn't right. Something was stirring, out of place, just plain wrong. She couldn't tell what it was, or how she knew something was amiss. Evelyn just knew. And it was urgent. She needed to wake Ren.

Evelyn sat up and started shaking Ren. "Ren, something isn't right. I can feel it."

"What's going on? It's not morning already, is it?"

"No, it's the middle of the night. But something's wrong."

"What is it?"

"I don't know, I just feel it. It has to be important."

Ren looked at his wife, and her seriousness instantly had him concerned. He pulled himself out of bed. "Let's go check it out."

Jacquelyn met them in the hall. "You two aren't very quiet. What are you doing awake?"

"Something is wrong," Evelyn replied. "I feel it. Come look with us."

They made their way to the balcony and peered out over the meadow. There was nothing to be seen in the inky darkness.

"Do you have any idea where or what it is?" Ren asked Evelyn. She shook her head but didn't stop peering into the darkness.

Jacquelyn was still groggy. "I think we should just go back to sleep."

Evelyn was tired, too. Maybe she was just too anxious about everything.

Ren put a finger to his lips and motioned for them to be quiet. Everyone was still, listening, feeling, looking. And then they heard it. Or felt it. A steady drumming, a rolling, thundering, rhythmic sound, vibrating deep through the ground from a distance, shaking right up the walls of the castle, through the floors, and up through their feet.

"What's going on, Ren?" Evelyn whispered.

Ren closed his eyes and tried to see what was out there with his mind. He wanted to be wrong, wanted to tell everyone that it was safe to go back to bed. But he couldn't. Evelyn and Jacquelyn were staring at him, waiting desperately for an answer.

"Let's get ready to fight." Ren pointed to Jacquelyn. "Have the army ready." He turned and motioned to Evelyn. "Stick with me. We don't have much time."

45

Ren and Evelyn watched off the balcony as the army in the distance advanced. "What are we going to do?" Evelyn asked.

"I don't know." Ren had one hand on his head, reviewing all their options. "I don't know how much you can do to help us."

"Why not?"

"You can't kill an entire army the way you killed Virgo, it takes too long."

"We still have to try. I'll learn as we go." Evelyn looked out at the meadow. "Who is leading them? Why are they attacking us?"

At that moment, flames burst in front of Evelyn and Ren, causing them to stumble back from the heat. A tall woman, clothed in a dress that seemed to be made from the flames themselves, emerged from the fire. Ren gasped in recognition. The woman smiled. "Did you miss me, children?"

Evelyn grabbed Ren's arm. "Maserta?" she questioned.

"Good to know you've heard about me," Maserta gloated.

Evelyn started towards Maserta. Ren grabbed his wife's elbow protectively, pulling her to a stop.

"Ren." Evelyn pulled away from his grasp gently. "I have the feeling only the Queen of Light is going to be allowed to challenge the Queen of Darkness."

Maserta nodded. "That's right."

Evelyn moved towards Maserta and Ren sighed. He had to put faith in his queen. This was exactly what her power was for.

"Let's get this over with, shall we?" Maserta taunted. "Join me on the roof?" She disappeared.

Evelyn glanced back at Ren and smiled. "Don't worry. I've been trained by all the best."

Ty had trained Ren well, too, through example, and Ren believed in his Queen of Light.

Evelyn vanished, following Maserta to the roof. She was ready.

Immediately upon arrival to the rooftop, Evelyn pulled out her dagger and lunged at Maserta, throwing her off guard. The wicked queen hadn't expected Evelyn to be on the offensive. Her youthful spirit complimented Evelyn, even if she was less experienced than the evil queen.

Maserta drew swords into each of her hands from thin air. "Now we shall see who truly deserves to be ruler of this land." Maserta raised a shield over the roof, trapping Evelyn in and keeping any possible help out. A ring of fire blazed around them, continually shrinking, bringing the enemies ever closer to each other.

"There is only room for one ruler," Maserta challenged Evelyn. "Which one of us will it be?"

"Bring it," Evelyn smiled confidently with determination.

It was an epic battle of blades, each woman having different expertise to throw at the other. There was never a pause in their battle. Catch a breath and you very well may die.

At last Maserta gave Evelyn a hard blow and knocked her weapons out of her hands. In desperation, Evelyn leaped forward away from the fire, grabbing Maserta's wrists, thus forcing her to drop the swords.

The circle of fire was drawing closer. Evelyn felt her energy wearing thin.

Maserta was stronger. She bent Evelyn over backwards, forcing her closer to the flames. Evelyn struggled to break loose, but she couldn't get free. Maserta was stronger.

"You're so foolish for ever thinking you could beat me," Maserta chided. "Or purge your land of my kingdom. No one can influence the darkness. Heretrua will never overcome Scaolust."

The flames were getting closer, hotter. "The Queen of Light can influence darkness," Evelyn countered.

"You are only a girl," Maserta sneered. "No queen at all."

Maserta threw Evelyn into the flames. As she fell, Evelyn had one last idea. With all the strength she could muster, Evelyn turned the flames against their maker. She warped the circle around Maserta, and curled up in a ball, squeezing her eyes shut and covering her ears.

The explosion that followed shook the foundations of that world. Fire and light shot straight up into the air, and rained down on the armies. When Evelyn finally dared to uncurl, Maserta was gone. All that remained of the battle was a large black circle on the rooftop.

Evelyn steadied herself on her feet, went to the edge of the roof, and looked out over the battling armies. She was so exhausted. Wiping out the rest of the kingdom looked impossible right now, but Heretrua couldn't do it without her.

How much longer Evelyn's magic would last was debatable. She knew she needed to let it rest and refill if she was to have any chance at succeeding, so she set off to join the battle on foot.

She fought her way to Ren and Jacquelyn, conserving as much strength as she could until she reached them and was able to put a bubble of protection around them.

"You beat Maserta?"

"Yes, but now what? We're still over powered and I'm worn out."

"You still have to try, Evelyn, it's our only way out."

"But how?"

Ren formed a glowing ball of energy above their heads. "We'll help." Jacquelyn joined in and nodded at Evelyn. She took a deep breath. They could do this.

Once the Queen's magic was added to Ren and Jacquelyn's it glowed bigger and brighter than ever before. "Okay. Now take care of it," Ren said, pointing to the Scaolust castle.

Evelyn let the shield dissolve and moved the swirling power higher, adding to it more and more. She pulled everything she had left from deep inside herself, aimed at the castle, and let the magic loose.

It shot across the meadow straight into Scaolust's castle. The burst of light following the explosion was blinding. The dark castle crumbled and crashed into the ground into a massive pile of black bricks, rumbling the earth even to where Evelyn was standing.

The fighting seemed to cease right then as both armies felt the shock of the castle falling. "You've been defeated," Evelyn proclaimed. "Maserta is dead and your castle is demolished. Surrender before the same thing happens to you."

Evelyn's command echoed across the battlefield until Heretrua had all of Scaolust's army either captive or dead.

Too exhausted to hold herself up, Evelyn felt Ren pull her into his arms. "We did it Evelyn," he whispered in her ear. "You did it. Scaolust is gone."

Evelyn leaned against him and as Jacquelyn joined them Ren wrapped an arm around her, too. There had never been a more dearly bought or hard earned moment in Evelyn's life.

The army was waiting silently for some word from their rulers. Ren addressed them.

"Gentlemen," he called out triumphantly. "Our victory is complete" Cheering erupted from the crowd and Jacquelyn chimed in, stepping forward.

"Now we will finally have peace and freedom, under the guidance and protection of Rennigan and Evelyn. Your king and queen." She turned to look back at her brother and his wife. "Rulers of Light."

Author's Note

Magic is not real.

I'm sure most of you are mature enough to understand that on your own, but there are those out there who do believe in magic in various forms, or at least something like it. I wanted to make it clear that I do not believe in magic, and it is not my intention to cause you to do so either.

It's sad though, isn't it? Magic is a favorite thing of mankind to imagine, to use in stories and in our imaginations. It's easy to yearn for its existence. That is why we authors use it in our stories. That's why we do many other things we do in our stories. We want our readers to yearn for things. Yearning is one of the most powerful feelings we can evoke in our readers. The fact that magic does not exist makes it perfect for our intentions. It teaches us true longing—longing for that which we can see and feel, but can never quite touch. Things such as magic and other worlds give us a taste of something beyond our grasp. It gives us a longing for something beyond this world and this life.

This book was inspired by the Chronicles of Narnia series. They have always been some of my favorite books. The Chronicles of Narnia had a fairy tale format, and they were certainly fantasy. Narnia does not exist, much as many of us would like it to. I've had many dreams of going to Narnia and meeting Aslan. It's the same longing. Lewis describes the kind of longing a fairy tale evokes as being different from normal stories like this:

It would be much truer to say that fairy land arouses a longing for [we] know not what. It stirs and troubles [us] (to [our] life long enrichment) with the dim sense of something beyond [our] reach and, far from dulling or emptying the actual world, gives it a new dimension of depth. [We] do not despise the real woods because [we] have read of enchanted woods: the reading makes all real woods a little enchanted.

How many of us have acted out our own stories, "played pretend," made up our own little imaginary worlds? Be it in the basement, the backyard, the park, the stage, or the woods, almost every child, and most adults, know what it is to create for oneself an imaginary world. As an author, it's my job. I get to play pretend and dream for a living. I get to live a thousand different lives in a hundred different worlds. And I get to share them with all of you.

I live on thirty acres of beautiful pasture land with a little wooded area, a huge barn, and a pond. The farmhouse I live in is over a hundred years old. I find things all the time around here that give me the sense of "fairy land" as Lewis put it. Every time I read a new story, it adds a whole new dimension to my own real world. Stories help us see the world in a new light. They teach us about the enchantment of our own world. Stories are like a lens through which we can begin to see the world in its true form.

However, we must be careful. As an author, I also have a duty to all of you. That duty is to tell you the truth. I can give you true ideas about the world and I can also feed you lies. If you believe that all literature out there is good, you are walking a dangerous path. People will try to lie to you, and they will try to give you a false view of the world.

You see, life is not just fun and games. It's not just good all the time. It's also hard. There is evil lurking in the dark parts of the forest, and bad guys are always trying to trump the good guys. It is important that you recognize that both exist, and important that you can distinguish which is which. Sometimes fantasy makes the lines more clear, sometimes it blurs them. I hope to make the lines clear. Good is good, and evil is evil, although in a really intriguing plot line, and in real life, it often gets hard to see the lines of what is truly evil because it is well disguised.

The truth I am trying to teach you in my story is this; longing, yearning for beautiful, perfect, wonderful things beyond our grasp, is healthy. Magic is not real, but it is a useful tool in teaching us this longing. And fairy land, or Heretrua, is my way of showing you how to see the enchantment in our own world. Because it is there. There is always evil lurking, but that doesn't mean there isn't good, true goodness, just waiting to be found and unfolded.

Don't spend your life hiding from the darkness. Spend it reveling in the light. In the beauty that is our reality. And keep searching, keep grasping, for that beauty beyond our reach. Though we can never fully understand it, the more we search, the more we will find. Happiness and truth do exist, even beyond this life, if only we will open our eyes.

Special Thanks

First and foremost, the fullness of my gratitude, small though it may be in comparison to that which I owe Him, goes to God. Without Him, I am nothing.

Second, thanks to all of you for reading my book! I hope you loved it. An author without an audience is just a hermit.

My mother is by far the best mother ever. My biggest fan and writing coach, she set aside much of her own work and personal pursuits to make my dream come true. Her unwavering belief in me even when I didn't believe in myself is priceless.

My whole family is always there for me and has put up with a LOT from me during the writing of this book. Daddy, Jerad, Macy, Aubrey, Halle, and Kinsley—even though you may have questioned my sanity multiple times, thanks for sticking with me. I love you!

Josiah and Reed Pringle, your swords are awesome, as are you. If anyone should win an award for supportive and generally awesome friends, it's you. I couldn't do without your advice and expertise in the areas I know nothing about, so thanks for keeping me realistic in the midst of my dreaming.

Grace Flesher, you are such a wonderful friend; your support and inspiration means the world to me. You understand fantasy and you know good literature. Thank you for believing in me and being excited with me.

Kellie Eastham, thank you for your gorgeous pictures! Our photo shoot was so much fun, you did a wonderful job capturing my true spirit.

Kenzie Holzinger, thank you for your incredible cover art! It wraps up and presents this labor of love perfectly. You are a Godsend and have given me an amazing gift. I look forward to getting to know you better and working with you much more in the future.

Abby Baker and Elizabeth Taylor, thank you for always supporting me and being excited for and with me.

Kathie Scott, ever since I met you, you've understood my passion. Thank you for all the little gestures that show you care.

Jeannette Annis, thank you for cheering on a girl you barely know. You were the first person to read through one of my entire stories. Your feedback encouraged me to keep growing. Your surprise visit will forever be one my my favorite memories!

Ulla Kesler, your excitement is contagious. You bring out the best in me, and you've helped me become comfortable and confident in who I am, which is important for an introvert like me.

Amy Hannig, it's hard to find people with undying enthusiasm like yours. Your smiles and hugs make my day. You have such a beautiful heart. Thanks for being my biggest fan and for investing in me. PHC will always be the place that had me first.

Grace Gillaspy, thank you for volunteering your talent and for giving me my first glimpse of my book actually becoming a reality.

Paris Beacon News staff, I haven't even personally met all of you yet, but you've been a tremendous encouragement and support to me. I'm so blessed to be able to write with you.

Andrew Pudewa, thank you for teaching the IEW courses. They've made me a better writer than I ever would have been without them.

Andrew Clements, you started this whole thing with "A School Story." I've never read a book of yours I didn't love, and I doubt I'll ever outgrow them.

To all my other friends and family, you have been so supportive and encouraging to me in all the little things you do. If I thanked all of you for everything I've ever been grateful for, it would be another book. Just know that all of those "little" things pile up to be a landslide of love in the end.

I also drew inspiration from my favorite television show, My Little Pony. Don't question it. The writers of that show pack tons of truths into a crazy show about talking magic ponies.

Lastly, Aubrey, Genneviera is you. You are Genneviera. The relationship I hope to continue developing between her and Evelyn is that of mine and yours. I am so blessed to have you as my sister and my friend, my little blonde buddy. You're my Thor, I'm your Loki, you're my Obi Wan, I'm your Anakin, you're my John, I'm your Sherlock. Don't know what I'd do without ya, kid. Probably still have my sanity. What a boring life that would be.